Got 'til it's Gone

Got 'til it's Gone

Larry Duplechan

ARSENAL PULP PRESS
Vancouver

ARSENAL PULP PRESS
Suite 200, 341 Water Street
Vancouver, BC
Canada V6B 1B8
arsenalpulp.com

This is a work of fiction. Any resemblance of characters to persons either living or deceased is purely coincidental.

Text design by Bethanne Grabham
Cover design by Shyla Seller
Cover photograph by Tom Hernandez, BlueMoon Stock

Printed and bound in Canada

Library and Archives Canada Cataloguing in Publication
Duplechan, Larry
      Got 'til it's gone / Larry Duplechan.

ISBN 978-1-55152-244-9

      I. Title.

PS3554.U585G68 2008   813'.54   C2008-904093-7

For Phil and Chris.

Part I
Tsunami

1.

I suppose the whole tsunami thing should have given me a clue; should have served as an epic reminder that you never know when life is just going to swoop down and wash you away. I mean, just think of those people, 200,000-plus of them—Indonesian, Indian, Thai—they never even saw it coming.

And of course, like most people, after I'd heard about the near-biblical devastation-and-death festival (on TV, in the *LA Times*, on the little LCD news screen in the elevator in my office building), I spoke in hushed, respectful tones about the total unpredictability of life. As I wrote my check to the Red Cross to aid the tsunami survivors, I paid the requisite lip service to how you just have to *carpe* the freakin' *diem* because one never knows, do one? Just as I'd done in 2001 after 9-11, after watching all the airplane-meets-large-building replays I could stand without putting my head in the oven and calling long distance to make sure all my East Coast friends were still in one piece. But now it was early May, and the nine-point-oh earthquake/ killer tsunami combo had been served way back in December (the day after my forty-eighth birthday, which I realize is apropos of nothing), and now all the talk was about the John Paul II Dead Pope Tour, how Marcia Cross of *Desperate Housewives* wasn't really a lesbian after all, and whether or not Macaulay Culkin was really going to take the stand at the Michael Jackson trial; frankly, I'd pretty much slipped back into the land of Same-Old-Same-Old. So, no: I didn't see it coming. My own personal tsunami caught me with my knickers down.

The call came at 7:45 p.m. I know this for a fact because, quite by coincidence, I had just removed my watch—the basic black Movado my late husband Keith had given me for our tenth anniversary, a whole mess of years ago. Spring had sprung and the evening was a warm one in Los Angeles and vicinity—even in Santa Monica, where close proximity to the Pacific usually rendered air conditioning unnecessary—and my arm was sweaty and itchy under the watch. I'd glanced at the time as I set the Movado down on the table—7:45—golden darts forming a wide angle on the watch's shiny black face.

It had been a thoroughly pleasant Friday evening up till then. I was at Maggie and Daniel's house. Maggie and Daniel Sullivan: my best buds for—I don't know—fifteen or something years. Odd as it may seem for a middle-aged black homo to be best friends with a couple of white, married, breeder types; that particular little org chart points to Crockett Miller. I'd met Crockett back in the early 80s: a pocket-sized blond stud with a smile like a halogen lamplight and a booty that brought tears to my eyes (like a summer sunset or a Billie Holiday ballad); he was a former college gymnast, sometime actor, pseudonymous author of ladies' romance novels, and off-and-on fuck buddy of mine for a couple of years or so in the late 70s-early 80s.

Crockett was the first person I ever knew to test HIV-positive, back in 1985. He died of AIDS in late '89. The young 'uns don't seem to believe it's true, but back in the day, most people didn't *live* with AIDS. Mostly they died. During Crockett's illness, I got to know (and eventually came to love) Maggie and Daniel. They were already Crockett's best friends by the time I met them; they were his family, really, after his mother decided she just wasn't up to it. Crockett and Daniel had been tight friends for years, had done theater together in their twenties, roomed together for awhile, I think; and when Daniel met, wooed, and finally wed Maggie Taylor, Crockett made three. Just between you and me, I always suspected Crockett and Daniel had been more than just buddies at some point; but I've got no proof, no blackmail photos—just a hunch.

As Crockett's condition nose-dived, first slowly, and then in an alarming fast-forward, we took care of him as best we could (Maggie and Daniel, and I): we drove him to and from doctor's appointments; and later, we took turns sitting in his hospital room through the nights, so if he woke up in the wee smalls and needed something, one or the other of us would be there. They really amazed me, Maggie and Daniel did. They'd only been married for three years or something at that point, and there they were, practically giving their whole lives over to their friend. Now, I've seen gay men do this for other gay men and I've seen some lesbians do the same for male friends or family members—but never the straight friends. From what I've seen, the straight friends generally brought an ostentatious bouquet of flowers and a big Mylar balloon on their first-and-only hospital visit, then dressed tastefully and wept audibly at the memorial service; but you couldn't count on them to be there to clean you up if you had an accident in your pajama bottoms. But Sully and Mags—well, the fact is Crockett actually died at their house: they'd rented a hospital bed and hospiced him in their home the last few weeks.

And by the time Crockett left us, I realized we had become family, too: Maggie and Sully and me. Oh, yes—at some point in the proceedings (and quite without his permission, please note), I had started calling Daniel Sullivan by his last name (or just Sully), because my mother's husband's name is Daniel and it was just one Daniel too many for me. And Sully doesn't seem to mind. Not that he's ever chosen to mention it, anyway.

I look back on it now and I can't believe how young we all were, just barely into our thirties. Makes me feel old. Lately, most things make me feel old.

Anyway, that fateful Friday evening, I was sitting cross-legged on Maggie and Sully's Persian-rug-covered living room floor, pleasantly buzzed (a half-finished flute of Mumm sat in a puddle of its own sweat on the glass-top coffee table). Los Lonely Boys were singing "How far is heaven?" from the in-wall stereo speakers. And I was pretty sure I was going to domino on my next turn, and get whatever points Sully and his son Ethan were holding. (I'd taught the Sullivans how to play Dominoes—or "Muggins," anyway—the one Dominoes game I know, and have known seemingly from the cradle, the one where you score multiples of five; they were all more or less addicted.)

"Little Love," Sully said to Maggie, "is this the radio? Good music." Sully was massaging his wife's recently-pedicured right foot with one long-fingered hand, his three remaining faux-ivory dominoes face-down on the table and seemingly forgotten. He had knocked twice that round and, as often happens when he's losing, he'd largely lost interest in the game. He scratched the tip of his nose (smallish and straight with a slight flare at the nostrils—the perfect white guy nose) with the hand not full of his wife's foot. As usually happens at least once every time I see him, I was struck anew by Sully's good looks—he was the personification of tall, dark, and handsome. Very Christopher Reeve, post-Superman, pre-tragic horseback riding accident.

"Johnnie brought the music," Maggie said. She was seated across the table from me (looking casual but elegant in khakis and a white blouse), staring down at the two dominoes she had left, tugging absently at a jaw-length lock of her straight blond hair, her bangs obscuring her eyes like a window shade.

"Custom-made CD," I said, scratching at a chronic dry, itchy spot near the top of my nearly-hairless head (my weekly self-administered buzzcut was only about an hour old). "I made a playlist especially for this evening: a smooth jazz cut for Mags, followed by classic rock for Sully, something at least semi-current for Ethan, and Joni Mitchell for me: jazz, oldie, VH1, Joni. Just play, Mags. I'm gonna domino."

Maggie picked up one tile, put it down, then tapped the tabletop a couple of times with a red-lacquered fingernail, picked the same tile back up again, and said, "Well, no matter how long I look at these effing things, I can't score."

"Then *play*, already," her husband said, apparently eager to move on to the next hand.

"Shut up," Maggie sing-songed back, never lifting her eyes from the table and her two remaining tiles. Finally, she said, "I was wrong." With a smile on her lips and a little flourish of her wrist, she placed a domino down at the end of the longest line of tiles and said, "Fifteen!"

"No way!" Ethan said, his nose nearly touching the table as he counted the little multi-colored dots, checking Maggie's arithmetic.

"Fiddeeeen!" Maggie shouted, holding up her diminutive right hand as if taking an oath.

"Nice job, partner," I said, reaching across the table to slap Maggie's palm with my own. Ethan retrieved the stub of a pencil from behind his right ear and recorded his mother's score on the slip of pale-pink paper (from one of Maggie's personalized scratch pads) he was using as a scorecard.

Now it was Ethan's turn to stare at his two remaining tiles, cupped in the palm of his hand. He muttered, "Shit, shit, shit." Maggie gave him a little pinch on his black-T-shirted shoulder and said, "Language."

"Sorry, Mom," Ethan said, and looked at the tiles in his hand, then at the board, then turned his head to the left and glanced at me. "You're getting bigger," he said. "Your guns are bigger and you're getting a big neck."

"Thank you for noticing," I said, more pleased than I chose to let on. "Now play."

"You juicing?" Ethan said. He laid his two dominoes facedown on the table and cocked his head to one side, appraising me.

"No, cherub, I am not on steroids," I said. "I've split my routine, I'm lifting heavier, and every day I consume more animal protein than the entire country of India has ever *seen*. Play."

"Looks good," Ethan said, leaning toward me and tracing a vein on my forearm with his long, pale forefinger, his skin like cream against the house-blend coffee of my own. The corners of his lips rose in an insinuating smile. Recently fifteen years old (born one year to the day after Crockett Miller died), Maggie and Sully's only child had come out to his parents as bisexual at the age of twelve. And like all teenage boys, he was little more than a life-support system for a 24/7 boner. Possessing a reasonable facsimile of his father's matinee-idol face and of his mom's golden blond hair (which he wore straight and shoulder length, like one of Cher's wigs), Ethan was somewhat overly aware of his own beauty, and an inveterate tease. I imagine he flirted with mail boxes and fire hydrants just to keep in practice.

"Maggie," I whined, making a big show of leaning away from Ethan's touch, "your son is distracting me."

"That was the general idea," Ethan said, working his fingertips up under the short-short sleeve of my Calvin Klein cotton-Lycra-blend tee.

"Stop molesting your uncle Johnnie," Maggie said in her habitual even tone. "He's about to domino."

"I thought you were looking particularly sturdy of late," Sully said, then knocked back the last swallow from a glass of Chianti. "What's that about?"

"Just wanted to put on a little more muscle," I said. "Five foot eight and 147 pounds struck me as a physique for a boy, not a middle-aged man. I thought I'd try for maybe a nice, lean one-seventy." I thumped Ethan on the shoulder and said, "You ever gonna play?"

Ethan said, "When I'm ready. What do you weigh now?"

I confessed, "I seem to have stalled at one-sixty-two."

"You already had a great body," Sully said. "Why this need to further humiliate me?" He made a sour face at me and gave the belly beneath his white Lacoste shirt a playful pat, as if it were an unruly but beloved pet. It wasn't a bad belly for a fifty-year-old straight man, but it was definitely a belly where, once upon a time, there had dwelt a six-pack of abs.

I said, "I thought it might give me a slightly more masculine look."

"You going on the downlow?" Maggie said, a self-satisfied little smile on her face.

Ethan laughed a puppy-bark of a laugh as Sully asked, "Going on the *what*?"

"I'll explain it to you later, Dad," Ethan said, chuckling.

I leaned in toward Maggie and said, "You've been waiting for *weeks* to use that term in a sentence, haven't you?" Maggie nodded, stifling a giggle. "Well, as it happens, going on the downlow presupposes that one is able to pass for straight. Which has never been an option for me."

"Got *that* right," said Ethan.

I poked my tongue out at Ethan, like a third-grader on the playground.

"Still and all," Sully said, "those of us who can't imagine having to try to gain weight, can't help wondering why."

Suddenly Maggie's eyes widened. "Oh my God," she said, motioning as if to reach across the table for me, then stopping herself, "you're not sick, are you?"

"No, no, no, I'm fine," I said. "It's just that—" Did I really want to go into this? It was silly and vain, and I had never actually verbalized it before and, besides, I was about to domino. Finally, I said, "The thing is, I'm forty-eight years old."

"I'm going on fifty-one," said Sully, picking up one of his dominoes and looking at the face of it as if it might have changed its spots since the last time he'd looked. "What's your point?"

I said, "It's different for straight guys, Sully."

"What's different?" he asked.

"I'm gonna tell ya," I said. "You asked me, so I'm gonna tell ya." I glanced at Ethan, then turned to Maggie and said, "Parental discretion is advised." Ethan executed an eye roll involving his entire head and neck.

"You gonna get graphic?" Maggie asked. She was, I suspect, less concerned for her young but disconcertingly sophisticated son than for herself: her threshold for discussions of man-on-man action was not particularly high.

"I don't think so."

I looked to Sully, who shrugged and said, "You may proceed."

Suddenly wishing I'd prepared a PowerPoint presentation (title slide: "Johnnie Ray Rousseau's Theory of Urban Gay Male Aging"), I began.

So, here's the thing: I am forty-eight years old. In less than two years, a year from this Christmas I'll be fifty. Now, you may have heard how fifty is the new forty. This is (as they say in the scientific community) a total crock. You know who made that shit up? Somebody who'd just turned fifty. Fifty is fifty. It's middle age, big-time middle age, and that's if you're planning to live to be a hundred.

Sully nodded and said, "Granted," then shrugged and added, "So what's *gay* got to do with it?"

"You gonna let me do this?" I said. Sully put his hands up in an ex-actor's pantomime of acquiescence, and I continued.

Now, once a gay man turns fifty, he's basically got three choices as far as his physical image, the image he's likely to convey for at least the next twenty years of his life (if he's lucky enough to last that long). Those three choices are:

1. *The Troll.* As the name alone should tell you, this is by far the least attractive alternative. As just about everyone knows, youth and beauty are the coin of the realm in the Gay World (even more so than in the world at large), so there's no sin like being an ugly old 'mo.

Granted, everybody's somebody's Troll (to misquote Connie Francis). For a twenty-year-old twinkie, a handsome thirty-year-old gym bunny may be a Troll. But Troll isn't simply about chronological age. I've known men to go Troll in their late thirties, and men who never have, well into their seventies. Troll is about the ravages of time left to run amuck, with absolutely no effort put forth to slow down said ravages. I'm not talking about laugh lines around the eyes and a bit of a wattle at the neck. I'm talking about haystacks of untrimmed nose and ear hair and a pelican pouch under the chin. I don't mean middle-age spread, going from thirty-inch-waist Levi's to thirty-four's. I mean sagging manboobs lying atop a penis-obscuring belly, and a derriere with more pleats than a Japanese fan. As my mother says, if you keep saying good morning and good night, you're gonna get old. Age (or early death) is inevitable. Troll means you're just not trying. As God is my witness (clutching the dirty, half-eaten radish), I will *never* be a Troll.

2. *The Auntie.* Auntie isn't so much about physique as it is about attitude. It's about the sort of androgyny that can be charming, even sexy in a man of twenty-five—fluttering hand motions, a pronounced sibilance, the habit of calling absolutely *everyone* "Myrna"—but that can prove to be considerably less charming and sexy in the same man twenty-five years later. You can spot the Auntie at any gay bar on any Sunday afternoon (for brunch, if such bar happens to be appended to a restaurant), usually in the company of one or more brightly-colored cocktails and one or more fellow Aunties—they often travel in gaggles. He may be round-bodied or willowy, but you can bet your lunch money he's wearing a loud, loose-fitting Hawaiian-print shirt (the caftan of the early twenty-first century) and probably some large-ish jewelry (in the western United States, usually silver-and-turquoise jewelry).

Unlike the Troll, the Auntie is generally quite well groomed—look closely and you may detect just a bit of judiciously-applied foundation makeup, and it's better than even money that his hair has never actually *been* that color.

Also unlike the Troll, the Auntie is often lots of fun to be around, especially if you, too, have been in the company of one or more brightly-colored cocktails. The Auntie is witty, knows every Broadway ballad ever written (not just the chorus, but the verses, as well), and (again unlike the Troll) will usually apply his hand to a younger man's knee, thigh or *tuchus* (all the while calling him "Sweetie"—the Auntie calls absolutely *everybody* "Sweetie") only after said younger man has given some cue, verbal or non-verbal, that he might, in fact, welcome such attention, or at the very least, tolerate it.

Left to my own devices, given that I have been cursed with my mother's mid-alto speaking voice, that I could recite the screenplay to *All About Eve* in its entirety while in a deep coma, and my penchant for hand gestures bordering on semaphore, I would consider myself an Auntie just waiting to happen. And I suppose I could live with that. But my overwhelming preference would be to spend my silver years as:

3. *The Daddy.* The Daddy is exemplified by the sixty-year-old dude with slate-grey hair in a military cut strutting down Santa Monica Boulevard on Pride Day wearing a pair of black jeans, a white tank undershirt, work boots, and a handsome man thirty years his junior, and it totally works because this old guy is so effing hot. While there are, of course, exceptions, carrying off the whole Daddy look usually requires a certain amount of lean muscle mass. A modest paunch is often permissible, but only with enough arm, chest, and shoulder to balance it out. With an impressive enough set of guns, you can make

a habit of calling absolutely *everybody* "Sweetie," and still be a Daddy. This is the goal to which I currently aspire.

Sully chuckled quietly but vigorously, his superhero shoulders shaking. He finished off with a sound halfway between a sigh and a wheeze and said, "My friend, you are truly disturbed."

I shrugged. "So tell me something I don't know."

"Sounds a bit mean-spirited," Maggie said.

Another shrug. "I don't make the rules."

"Bro," Ethan touched me lightly on the forearm, his eyebrows raised in a parody of grave concern, "you are seriously vain."

I made a lemon-sucking face at him and said, "Glass houses, Junior. Now, *play*, already."

I unbuckled the band of my Movado, glanced at the time (7:45), and set the watch down on the tabletop, when from across the room my cell phone shouted, "Flavor *Flav!*" the ring tone I had downloaded from *vh1.com* and, in a spasm of silliness for which I have no excuse whatsoever, assigned to my mother (who wouldn't know Flav if all the members of Public Enemy were sprawled across her bed in their respective birthday suits).

"Oh, shit," I said.

"What is it?" Maggie asked.

"Something's wrong."

"Because your cell phone rang?" said Ethan, raising a blond eyebrow.

"It's my mother's ring tone," I explained to the room in general. "My mother calls me once a week, early Sunday evening, between six and seven—after her dinner and before *60 Minutes*." I pushed myself up from the floor, bashing my knee on the edge of the table on the way (I said "Ow!" and my phone said "Flavor *Flav!*"). I quickstepped across the living room toward the antique church pew hunkered against the wall of the entryway (and used primarily in lieu of an entryway closet—coats are parked there when coats are necessary), speaking half to myself and half to the Sullivans: "A phone call from my mother at any other time can mean only one of two things: either somebody's dead or, best case scenario," I snatched the phone up from the seat of the pew, "somebody's dying."

I flipped the phone open ("Flavor *Fl*—").

"Mom?" I said, the pitch of my voice shooting up into castrato country (an Auntie voice if there ever was one).

"John, it's Daniel." My mother's husband had never called me on the telephone, much less from my mother's cell phone, in the eighteen years of their marriage. I heard myself saying, "Sweet Jesus," before Daniel had finished saying (in the resonant bass-baritone voice I have always envied), "I've got some bad news." It occurred to me that I might fall down, but then I realized that I had already sat down on the pew. Daniel said, "I would have called sooner, but Clara couldn't find her address book and it was hours before either of us remembered that, of course, you're programmed into her cell phone. We've been a little bit scattered."

I waited, listening to my pulse pound in my temples.

"John," he repeated. My actual first name is Johnnie: Johnnie Ray Rousseau, happy to make your acquaintance and how are all *your* folks? Dr Daniel Weinberger is the only person in my life who insists on calling me John. "Are you there?"

"Yes," I said, "I'm sorry, Daniel. Tell me. What, what is it?"

"It's your mother, John."

"Oh, for fuck's sake, Daniel," suddenly I was shrieking like a bad actress in a B horror flick, "I didn't think you were calling to give me bad news about Condoleezza Fucking *Rice*, now, would you please just *tell* me!"

"I need you to calm down, John." Daniel was now using his Medical Professional Voice, the one I imagine he uses when assuring a patient that testing HIV-positive was definitely *not* a death sentence or encouraging another to remember to use a condom, every single time. "Breathe, John. I need you to breathe right now."

"All right, Daniel. I'm breathing." Which was a lie. I was actually scratching a groove into the finish of the pew with my thumbnail and clenching my teeth against the painful pounding in my head, a merciless assault by a six-inch-tall bloody-red imp wearing oversize brass knuckles, snickering as he executed rapid punching-bag work with my brain.

I don't know if Daniel believed me or not, but after a moment, he said, "Clara has a brain tumor, John." The imp was striking a boxing bell in my ear, over and over. Through the ringing in my head, I may have heard Daniel add, "It's growing. And, because of its position against her brain, it's inoperable."

The imp tossed the boxing bell aside and pulled a switchblade out of a magic pocket in his naked hip, a knife longer than he was tall, and slit me up the middle like a pig, pubic bone to breastbone. I watched my vital organs tumble, steaming and shiny pink, into his little red hands.

"Please tell me this is your idea of a joke," I said.

The imp yelled, "You fuckin' *WISH!*" and disappeared in a puff of red smoke, leaving me only the sound of his cackling laugh and a brain-shredding headache the likes of which I had never dreamed existed.

"I'm sorry," Daniel said.

I heard a sound of abject heartbreak, a wheezing, rasping sound of the sinuses and throat, all saltwater and mucus: Daniel was weeping. I said, "Shit." It was the only thing that came immediately to mind.

I heard Daniel sniff and hiccup and finally say, "Yeah."

"I'll be there as soon as I can."

"Clara said to tell you not to. She doesn't want you to make the drive."

"Do you always do what Clara says?" I asked.

He paused a moment, sniffed again. "Pretty much."

"I guess it's a husband thing," I said. "But she's my mother."

I flipped the phone closed and looked up to find Ethan squatting next to me. From the expression on his face, I must have looked like seven different kinds of hell. He rested a long hand on my knee, squeezed softly.

"What is it, Johnnie?" he asked.

It took a moment. I couldn't find the words. I suddenly understood why people in holy roller churches, in the throes of spiritual ecstasy, speak in tongues; resorting to rhythmic clicks and nonsense syllables, a sort of extraterrestrial scat-singing understood only by themselves and God. There are times when earthly language simply does not suffice. Finally, I managed to say, "Tsunami."

2.

It was nearly ten o'clock when I finally got onto Interstate 10 heading toward Palm Desert. I was a few minutes getting out of the Sullivans' house, what with recounting my conversation with Daniel, accepting my friends' individual and collective words of (in order of appearance) surprise, concern ("Bro, that totally sucks," offered by Ethan, was my personal favorite), and encouragement; followed by their respective hugs, and advice that I drive carefully. I must have driven home with sufficient care, as I did make it from Santa Monica to Mar Vista (the nearby, considerably less expensive neighborhood where I lived) in one piece; though I honestly couldn't have said with any certainty whether I'd driven home or ridden a broomstick. I was pushing the button for the automatic garage door opener when it occurred to me that I remembered nothing of the drive home. It was as if I'd hit a crease in the space-time continuum.

The incessant banging and ringing in my head created a sort of white noise keeping conscious thought at a minimum as I dropped a few essentials (toothbrush and floss, contact lenses' case and all-in-one solution) into my shaving kit, then pushed it, along with a pair of jeans, a couple of basic white 2Xist T-shirts, and two pair each of jockey shorts and athletic socks into my electric-orange gym bag (a souvenir from a recent gay cruise to the Mexican Riviera). I filled an extra bowl of dry food and a second bowl of fresh water for my cats (two near-identical jet-black shorthairs whom I'd had the grandiose bad taste to name Amos and Andy) and scooped out the litter box. Amos (slightly larger and heavier than his brother, and the undisputed alpha cat) began munching immediately, batting kibble into his mouth with his right forepaw (an eating style I have yet to see employed by any other cat), crunching and smacking as I wrapped the clumps and droppings in newspaper. Andy meowed over and over, a sound as much like a car alarm as a cat, until I put the stinky newspaper bundle down, sat cross-legged on the floor, and tapped the middle of my chest with my hand. Andy answered our years-old signal, climbing into my lap. He curled himself into a lumpy circle of black fur, his head pushing into my lower belly, his unusually vigorous purr vibrating against my abs.

Through the ringing in my ears, the sound of crying seemed to come from somewhere outside myself, from another room, another house. It wasn't until later that it occurred to me what an odd collection of sounds must have been hanging in the air of my combination home office/cat sanctuary: the kibble crunching of one cat, the full-throated purring of another, and the middle-aged homosexual crying like a child with a bleeding boo-boo.

I gave myself over to weeping, wailing like someone from the Old

Testament (wherein people, according to the King James Version, "cried out in a loud voice"), crying until my throat hurt and a bib of wetness formed on the front of my shirt; until I was pretty sure I was all cried out, no tears left. Then I tapped Andy on the behind (our signal that it was time to leave Daddy's lap) and stood up. I pulled my shirt off and wiped my face and blew my nose with it while Andy meowed at me some more, and then I went to the bedroom for another shirt.

My usual soundtrack for the two-hour drive to Palm Desert is the Joni Mitchell playlist on my iPod: beginning with the original 1967 version of her classic "Both Sides Now" and ending with "Got 'Til It's Gone," the 1997 Janet Jackson jam featuring a sample from "Big Yellow Taxi." In average traffic, this playlist gets me from my front door to my mother's, almost exactly. But two hours of Joni, goddess though she is, wasn't quite right for this particular drive. My mother was dying, and there was only one lady to get me to the desert without willfully driving myself over an embankment: Lady Day. I plugged the white rectangular widget into the auxiliary input I'd had installed in the stereo of my 2000 Honda Accord (to the tune of 300 bucks, and worth every penny), thumb-tickled the click wheel to select the Billie Holiday listing and then "All." The 5,050-odd tracks whirring in my favorite gizmo's teensy twenty-gig hard drive included the entire three-CD set of *Billie Holiday—The Legacy 1933–1958*, seventy songs and over three hours' worth of the greatest jazz vocalist ever to draw breath, exhale music, and destroy herself with illegal poison way too young (Billie died at forty-four—four years younger than I was). Gil Scott-Heron could call on Lady Day and John Coltrane to wash his troubles away, but you can keep Coltrane, as far as I'm concerned: Billie's all I need. I clicked "Play," and as the descending clarinet run at the beginning of "Your Mother's Son-In-Law" (1933, Billie's very first recording) wriggled its way across my car's interior, I backed out of the garage, feeling about as good as a man could expect to feel, so soon after having been eviscerated by a cartoon imp.

I can only suppose that news of a mother's terminal illness would be devastating for just about anyone. So please note: I don't mean to imply that my pain is bigger and badder than yours, or that I love my mother deeper and wider than you love yours. All I mean to say is that Clara and I are tight—always have been. She has always been the first to own up to our peculiar bond. "I love both my children," she used to say back when she had two of them, prior to my younger brother, David's, premature departure from this earthly plane, "but there's something about the first." And in my humble opinion (or IMHO, as they say online), as mothers go, Clara is the shit. Ethan assures me that "the shit" is still the current jargon for what seemingly minutes ago was called "the bomb."

True, we've had our bad days, Clara and I. Hell, we've had our bad *years*. For instance, the couple of years immediately following my graduation from college, when we didn't speak. At all. At that point, Clara was still riding the high horse of her Church of God in Christ upbringing and insisting that homosexuality was sinful and godless and just plain wrong, by definition, because the Bible told her so, and I just didn't have time for that—drop me a line when you get over it. Which she did, eventually. I imagine it can be tough on a mother when her first and favorite son turns out gay. When Clara found out, she told me it was like hearing that I'd been killed in a car crash. I was seventeen years old. That was definitely one of our bad days. But to her credit, she did mellow considerably over time. As, I like to think, did I.

But over the arc of my life, I'd have to say that as mothers go, a boy could do worse. A lot worse.

I have asked my mother more than once, where and from whom she learned the fine art of mothering. Who, I wonder, instilled in her the notion that her children always came first? Always. Before husband or marriage, before family or friends, before her own health, physical comfort or happiness. She'd shrug, shake her head slowly, "I don't know," she'd say, "maybe it was the Lord." Which, I guess, is as good an explanation as any. Basic maternal instinct, some might argue. Animal instinct, even—mother housecats have been known to pull their kittens from burning buildings, even as Mama Kitty's own ears are being singed off. What mother *doesn't* put her children's lives, welfare, health, and happiness before her own? Of course, the answer to that question is: lots of them.

My mother, née Clara Jane Johnson, has left me with little patience for a mother, any mother, who leaves the father of her children because the thrill is gone, or because she needs to "find herself," or because, by golly, she's just not happy. If such a mother happens to be a friend or friendly acquaintance of mine, I will smile an understanding half-smile, pleat my brow into a mask of sympathy, nod, and say, "Sure, I can see that," while above my head floats a fluffy, comic-book thought bubble bearing words along the lines of: "Happy? Why, you selfish cow! How dare you sit there, prattling on about your happiness? Your happiness is of no significance whatsoever: for the love of God, you're somebody's *mother!*" This very well might mean that I am an asshole. So be it. It's not my fault: it's Clara's.

"I'd take anything but a beating for my children," Clara has said to me, many times. Like most people of a certain age (and I myself have reached that age), if Clara has said something, told you a story, mouthed some platitude once, chances are she's done so several hundred times. But it's true. I know for a fact that during her twenty-one-year marriage to my father, she took a good deal of what used to be called "guff" from him; not so much because he was her husband but because he was the father of her children: her two ashy-legged, long-headed, rusty-butt boys.

Lance Rousseau, my late father, was roughly the same age (born in the early 1930s) and hailed from the same general geography (the American South) as that famous wife-batterer, Ike ("yeah, I hit her") Turner; and while my dad never did hit my mother (Clara has claimed she'd kill him if he ever did—and I don't doubt her for a moment), I don't imagine he would have considered it particularly out of line if he had. And he was (in fact) known to belittle, shout down, intimidate, threaten to leave, and otherwise mind-fuck his wife as he found appropriate. Still, as long as he took financial care of her children (and, almost incidentally, of her), kept a roof over their collective heads, kept their stomachs full, and refrained from physically striking her, Clara considered it her duty to stick it out. And so she did, until after I was grown up and on my own, and my brother David had died.

So (you may well ask), do I think every unhappy wife and mother should remain in an unsatisfying, unsatisfactory marriage for the sake of the children? Probably not, I will admit (if somewhat grudgingly). And it's certainly arguable that, being male and childless, I haven't the first clue what it's like to be a wife or a mother (happy or otherwise), and as such have only the most tenuous right to an opinion on the subject. But again, Clara's example is clear. She chose to stay with the father of her children, and with him she raised her two rusty-butts. And as for those children: might we not have been happier in a single-parent home than in one where the wife and mother was not

100 percent hap-hap-happy 100 percent of the time? As Clara's sole surviving (ostensibly adult) child, I can safely say: perhaps. That is, if we'd had any idea Mom wasn't happy; which we hadn't. Clara never allowed any issues she may have had with Lance to affect her kids. She was too busy keeping us in clean (if not always new) clothes, braising inexpensive cuts of beef into savory tenderness and finding the odd extra dollar from heaven-only-knows-where for such unnecessary (but in the longer run, infinitely rewarding) items as music lessons or the *Compton's Pictured Encyclopedia.* That's the kind of mother she was.

Which brings me back to the question: just where did a high school-educated girl from rural Southwest Louisiana, only twenty-one when she gave birth to her first child, learn to be a proper mother? Not (she claims) from her own mother, Mary Mayall Thibodeaux. By the time I knew my maternal grandmother, Mary was an old lady. I recall (and have a few snapshots to bear me out) a tall, angular, very black woman with naturally jet black, naturally straight hair and strikingly high, prominent cheekbones (hair and cheekbones apparently courtesy of a full-blood Seminole grandfather). Grandma Mary's deep rasp of a speaking voice (think Lauren Bacall with a head cold) was no doubt the product of the unfiltered Camel cigarettes she chain-smoked. (We didn't know enough to refer to them as "cancer sticks" in those days, but they would eventually take Grandma Mary's life.)

Mary gave birth thirteen times (which would turn any woman old); eleven of her children survived past infancy. I can only imagine that the struggle to keep body and soul together for six boys, five girls, a husband (Grandpa Sherman did backbreaking menial work in the nearby shipyards), and herself, in the Louisiana of the 1930s, 40s, and 50s must have made for a bone-bending, soul-crushing existence for the likes of Mary Thibodeaux. Like a medley of old Dolly Parton songs, Clara holds among her childhood memories: chicken feet for supper, an orange (and that's all) for Christmas, and an old whiskey bottle swaddled in rags improvised as a baby doll. Make no mistake, Grandma Mary loved her children and they loved her back (Clara has never fully recovered from Mary's passing, and it's been nearly thirty years), but she was far too occupied with finding something edible for the supper table to concern herself with (for example) whether or not her children were being properly exposed to higher culture.

By contrast, I remember that by the time I started school, I was already familiar with what I like to call "Your Classical Hit Parade": *The Nutcracker Suite, Peer Gynt,* the "Toreador Song" from *Carmen,* and the Christmas portion of Handel's *Messiah* by the Mormon Tabernacle Choir. I don't know if Clara bought or was given the scratchy LPs I played on my portable mono record player as a child; but more importantly: who, I wonder, gave her the idea that playing classical music in her home was worth the bother? Or that her children should learn to play at least one musical instrument each? Again, she'd plead, "I don't know." And then, after a moment of reflection, she'd say, "Maybe it was those Jews."

For a short time (a year maybe) before her first pregnancy and her wedding to my father (which events did, in fact, occur in that order), Clara was governess to two young sons of a wealthy Jewish family—maybe in Louisiana, maybe elsewhere (we'd never discussed it). I remember one small black-and-white snapshot of the young Clara, a remarkably pretty girl (Dorothy Dandridge could have played her in the movie, had such a movie been made in the 1950s—Halle Berry would be the obvious choice now), with deeply dimpled cheeks, shiny spit curls, and a pleated skirt; in the company of two little blond-headed boys in shorts, the smaller one (I'm guessing four years old) on her lap and the larger (maybe seven) standing up next to her on the bench she sits on. There are huge trees surrounding the bench—they could be in a park or maybe just a wealthy family's back yard. And I wonder: Did Clara hear her first Vivaldi on the hi-fi set in the home of this Jewish family (their name long ago forgotten)? Was the sturdy-legged older son taking clarinet lessons, perhaps reluctantly?

And suddenly, as I was approaching Redlands (the approximate halfway mark between my house and Clara's) as Billie sang "They Can't Take That Away From Me" backed by the Count Basie Orchestra, I wondered if Clara's memories of these Jewish children, this long-ago Jewish family (the Steinsteins, or whatever their name was) might have had anything to do with her choosing a big, red-headed, Jewish doctor as her second husband.

"She waited up for you," Daniel said, by way of greeting. "I told her not to, but you know how she is." He stood in the fifteen-foot door-way of the custom, ranch-style-on-steroids, gated-community home he shared with my mother, wearing a V-neck undershirt, jeans, and no shoes. I stepped inside, dropped my gym bag onto the terrazzo entryway floor, and extended my right hand to my—deep breath—stepfather. As I'd feared he might, Daniel caught me up in his beefy furbearing arms and hugged me close, crushing my face against his beard-stubbly neck, rendering me uncomfortably aware of his superior size, the shag rug of hair peeking out from under his shirt, and his not-altogether-unpleasant bodily scent. Yes, ladies and germs: my stepdaddy is a definitely a Daddy.

Every time I see Daniel Weinberger, MD (three or four times a year in recent years, generally around various holidays), I consciously have to remind myself that this man is my mother's husband. Not only is he, at fifty-two years old, seventeen years Clara's junior; he is only four years and a couple of months older than I am. And, the fact is, he's kind of hot. Tall and thick-muscled, and rather handsome in a nineteenth-century sort of way, deep-set blue eyes, a nose and chin with a valiant forward thrust: the face of a silent film hero—Francis X. Bushman in loose-fitting Levi's. I could imagine that face exchanging chaste, tightlipped kisses with Mary Pickford or Lillian Gish. (Oh, for Pete's sake, just Google them.)

The thought of him with my mother was not one I entertain often; both because, well, who would want to go there, of his own free will? And because—okay, if Dr Weinberger were queer, I'd *date* him. There—I've said it. I guarantee you, "Oedipal" does not *begin* to describe this.

When he finally released me from the hug, Daniel said, "She's in the music room." It was only then that I noticed there was music playing: piano chords, vaguely hymn-like, nothing I could recognize. I followed the sound out of the foyer and through what would have been the living room if Clara and Daniel's house actually *had* rooms (only the bedrooms and bathrooms had doors—the kitchen, dining room, living room, and "music room" were, in fact, one huge, open area (a "great room," as the interior designer set say) with only strategic furniture placement to separate them. Clara was seated at the Baldwin concert grand that designated the music room, half-hidden behind a ten-foot-high sculpture/painting: a seemingly random gathering of wood, canvas, and several clashing hues of oil paint, a *moderne* monstrosity. I liked most of the art in Daniel and Clara's house (which tends toward twentieth-century abstracts)—but this thing was a major exception. Clara stopped playing and tilted her head toward the sound of my approaching footsteps, then slid across the leather-upholstered bench and turned to face me, a smile lifting her lips.

She seemed even smaller than usual. Clara was just five feet tall, and around 140 pounds when she was at her heaviest (twenty years earlier, in bloated menopause). Suddenly, next to her huge piano, beneath her twenty-five-foot vaulted ceilings, my mother seemed particularly tiny, like a little girl wearing her mother's loose-hanging, ankle-length, pseudo African-print dress. Maybe it was her hair, cornrowed close to her head, looking rather like a black bathing cap, emphasizing her almond eyes and high cheekbones (there's that Seminole again). Maybe she had lost some weight. Maybe it was all in my mind.

"Hello, baby," she said, and lifted her arms to me. I barely managed "Ma" before doing a three-point collapse at her feet, my knees hitting the terrazzo floor hard. My face buried in her pseudo African-print lap, I found that I did, in fact, have tears left. Clara stroked the back of my head with one soft hand, and let me cry until I was finished. I sat up cross-legged (the terrazzo hard and cool against my ass), wrestled my handkerchief from the hip pocket of my jeans and blew a wet mess and a Bronx cheer into it, and said, "Here *you're* sick and you're comforting *me.*"

"I'm your mother," she said, as if that explained everything; and hell, maybe it did.

We just sat for awhile, me on the floor and Clara on the piano bench, for a couple of minutes. Then, she pointed her small, bare right foot out in front of her (a ballet student at the *barre*) and said, "Does this look like an old lady foot to you?"

I smiled for the first time in what seemed like years. "Mother of mine," I said, "absolutely nothing about you looks like an old lady." Which wasn't flattery, just the truth. She was five months shy of seventy, and the world was still waiting for Clara's face to show a wrinkle, just one. Without the benefit of Clairol, L'Oreal, or Shinola, she had exactly four grey hairs on her head—I'd named them Ruth, Anita, Bonnie, and June, after the Pointer Sisters. The foot I took into my hands and began to massage was smooth and soft, not a distended vein, not so much as a discolored toenail.

Clara closed her eyes, a little moan escaped her lips. She said, "That feels good." I massaged in silence for a minute or two, then said (to her foot, mostly), "So what am I supposed to do without you?"

"I'm *supposed* to go first," she said, calmly, evenly, as if we were talking about going on vacation. As if to remind me that one of her children had already preceded her toward the Big Light, she added, "I thank the Lord I *am* going first." She opened her eyes, looked intently down at me. "Have you lost weight?" she asked. While Clara had long since come to terms with what she persisted in calling my "lifestyle," she had a couple of dangling issues. One of them was the notion that "gay" was an acronym for "Got AIDS yet?" She just couldn't seem to shake the idea that I was destined to contract HIV at some point. Her asking if I'd lost weight—and she asked me each and every time I saw her—was code for "Sweet Jesus, tell me you're still healthy."

I tugged her big toe, then lowered her foot to the floor. "Mom, I've *gained* weight. I'm about twelve pounds heavier than the last time you saw me. I'm 162 pounds. I'm huge." I took hold of her left foot.

After a moment, she said, "So sue me for caring."

"You should never have married a Jew," I said, pressing into the ball of Clara's foot with my thumb. "You talk like a Borscht Belt comic."

She said, "You talk like Katharine Hepburn."

I had to smile. "*Touché.*"

"You *are* bigger," she said. "Got a big-ol' chest on you. All of a sudden you're a muscleman?"

"Fighting the aging process as best we can," I said, fiddling with her toes.

I heard a soft chuckle. She reached down, gave my left earlobe a little tug and sang, "You're so vain," like Carly.

"I come by it honestly," I said. I released her foot, daintily pointed my own foot at her (black Converse All Star sneaker and all) and said, "Does this look like an old lady foot to you?"

"*Touché*," she said, and we traded smiles.

Suddenly, Daniel was there, out of nowhere, startling us both with the unexpected sound of his basso voice: "It's late." Daddy come to send the kids to bed.

I got up from the floor, not without a brief argument from my right knee, extended my hand to Clara as if asking her to dance. She accepted it, and I assisted her rise from the bench. She wrapped her arms around my waist and hugged me hard, nearly knocking the breath out of me, and we held one another close for a long moment. I feared another attack of tears and pulled gently away. I hung an arm around Clara's shoulders and walked her to Daniel, as if giving her away in marriage. She tucked herself beneath her husband's arm, leaned her head against his chest. His body seemed to envelop her like a down-filled sleeping bag.

Daniel said, "The guest room is made up. Let me know if you need anything."

"I'll be fine," I said. "Good night, you two."

A bit later, I lay on the super firm king-size guest bed, struggling to find a comfortable position for my head on the too-soft goose down pillows. An inexplicable (and arguably inappropriate) hard-on complained between my legs, and I wished Dre was there. Not so much to deal with said boner (though he would, and remarkably well, God bless him), as to tuck himself against me, his back to my front, my arm around his flat belly, the sweet, warm odor of his dreadlocks in my face.

Dre! I suddenly remembered that I owed him a phone call; we had made a date for Saturday night to watch *I, Robot* on DVD and then make love—which I confess was our idea of a hot date. Not that Dre and I are dating, exactly. We're more like "friends with benefits," to use an expression I'm not fond of (though it's better than "fuck buddies," a term I like even less). I rolled over and picked up my cell phone from the nightstand (the LCD display shining like the Bat-Signal in the dark room) and thumbed Dre's number—I could punch his phone number, including the *82 to get past his caller ID, with my eyes shut, like Braille. He finally picked up on the fourth ring: "Hey."

"It's me," I said, but Dre kept talking: "I saw you the other night," he said, his balls-deep baritone thick with mischief and sex, "lookin' all good." Is the man high? I wondered—when it occurred to me (somewhat belatedly) that I was listening to my buddy's answering machine. I whispered an expletive and waited it out. "Gotcha," he said, and I heard his chuckle (*"heh-heh"*). "Leave a message and I'll hollah back." *Beeeeep.*

"It's me," I repeated. "I'm going to have to bail on tomorrow night. My mom's sick, and I'm spending the weekend in the desert. I'll call you when I get home. Sorry."

I was punching the pillows into submission when from the nightstand, Melle Mel said "Chakachakachaka—Chaka Khan?" Dre's ring tone.

"Hey, Shorty."

"Dre? Are you live or Memorex?"

"Just got home from rehearsal." Dre was choreographing an insistently homoerotic all-male modern dance recital for the John Anson Ford Theatre in North Hollywood: lots of muscular male bodies clad only in dance belts, performing *pas de deux* simulating steamy mansex over Moby recordings. A similar show he'd done the previous season had played to packed houses, despite—or perhaps due to—a review in the *Times* which described it as soft-core gay porn. "Sorry about your moms," he said. "Bad?"

"Brain tumor," I said. It tasted like a mouthful of dirt.

"Shit."

"Yeah. Sorry about tomorrow night."

"Call me when you get home," he said. "Okay? I don't have rehearsal Sunday night."

"I will."

"Ah'ma hit it: my ass is draggin'. This tryin' to keep up with a bunch of twenty-year-old dancers is fixin' to kill me. My shit is *old*."

He managed to make me smile. He usually did. "Watch how you toss the 'O' word around, okay, Mr Just Turned Forty?"

He chuckled his response: "*Heh-heh.* 'Night, Shorty."

"'Night."

Even talking about brain tumors, Dre's voice had added starch to my hard-on. My duty was clear: I slid out of bed and shuffled, half-blind, to the bathroom. I pulled my Neutrogena body lotion from my shaving kit, yanked a hand towel from the rack, and brought them back to bed with me. I'd sneak the towel into the laundry in the morning.

I awoke to the nearly intoxicating scents of coffee and bacon. I checked my wrist for the time, only to find I wasn't wearing my Movado. Neither was it on the night table. Apparently, I had left it at the Sullivans'. My cell phone's display said 9:07. I had slept nearly nine hours. In times of great stress, many people experience insomnia, but I sleep like a rock, grossly oversleep, basically go into shut-down. I rolled out of bed. Halfway to standing, a sharp pain in the vicinity of my right testicle (like a swift kick to the groin by a small child in tap shoes) shoved me back down onto the bed. Bent into a semi-fetal posture, I clenched my face against the throbbing, waiting for it to settle down to an ache.

It wasn't my first time. I'd been experiencing a nearly constant low-grade *schmertz* on or around my right nut for about a year. As I am the King of This Will Go Away By Itself, it took me nine months of daily discomfort and the occasional tap-shoe kick in the nads before I finally called the HMO for an appointment. Sasan Meradifar, my GP (a thirty-something-year-old Persian man so handsome I could swear he was actually an actor *playing* a doctor on some Iranian soap opera), tested my various bodily fluids for syph, clap, Chlamydia, and HIV and found none; he finger-diddled my prostate to the point where I felt like he owed me dinner at the very least, tested my PST, and declared my prostate normal-sized, lumpless, and, apparently, cancer free, then prescribed a six-week regimen of an unpronounceable anti-biotic, "just in case we missed something." He then suggested I take aspirin if things got too uncomfortable (meaning, I suppose, that I found myself praying for death), postulated that the pain might very well just up and move on all by itself (a prognosis worthy of me), then added that I was "at that age" when various body parts may begin to ache, sting, tingle, and/or go numb (and/or, I imagine, fall off) for no apparent reason and little hope of relief. Three months later as I sat bent double on my mom's guest bed with a right ball that hurt like a sumbitch on a nearly constant basis, I resolved to call the HMO to make an appointment for a second opinion.

I took a deep breath, pushed myself to my feet again, shuffled into the bathroom, and squeezed saline solution into my eyes (I had neglected to take out my contacts the night before, and now they felt like microscope slides). I pulled on the jeans I'd arrived in, and a fresh T-shirt, and made my slow, somewhat ginger, way to the kitchen.

Clara stood at the sleek black cooktop, spatula in hand, shoving bacon around a cast-iron frying pan she'd owned since before I was born (charcoal-black from a half-century of use and nonstick without the benefit of Pam). The white terry robe she wore nearly reached her toes and the sleeves were rolled up to her elbows—it obviously belonged to the husband. She had accessorized with a large floral-print oven mitt on her left hand. She was singing softly to herself a song I remembered from my childhood at the First New Ship of Zion Missionary Baptist Church in Inglewood, a literal stone's-throw from Watts: "None but the righteous / Shall see God."

I signaled my arrival with a theatrically loud clearing of my throat.

"Good morning, baby," she said, not turning from the grease popping in the frying pan. From behind, I kissed her cheek, wary of the hot spatters.

"Bacon?"

"What's it look like?" she said. (Among other things I have inherited from my mother for worse and/or better: high cheekbones, a singing voice, and a relentless penchant for sarcasm.)

I said, "Not particularly good for you at the best of times."

She scooted the pan off the fire with her mitt-wearing hand, turned off the burner, moved six slices of steaming, audibly sizzling bacon onto a plate covered with several layers of paper towel, and set the spatula down against the edge of the plate. She turned to me, pulled off the oven mitt, and said, "I may as well eat what I want now, don't you think?" I might have argued the point, but my mother was an intelligent grownup: she knew the case in favor of macrobiotics over bacon and eggs for a cancer patient as well as I did. "You want some coffee?" she said, tilting her head toward the restaurant-quality Braun coffee/espresso maker on the polished black granite counter. It was bigger than my first car, and likely more expensive.

"Lord, yes," I said, then I watched in silence as she poured me a mug of coffee from the ten-cup carafe. "Where's Daniel?"

"Hittin' golf balls," she said. She went to the refrigerator (like everything else in her kitchen, it was glossy, black, and seemingly built slightly larger than scale), retrieved a can of PET evaporated milk, and poured a healthy dollop of milk into the mug. "Much later in the morning and it'll be too hot to play." She put one, two, three heaping teaspoons of sugar into the mug, gave it a stir, and handed it to me. "He'll be back in a few minutes," she said. "I'll do the eggs and toast when he gets here, unless you're starving."

"I'm good for now," I said, and took a sip of the candy-sweet milky stuff. "Thank you." Normally, I would have already knocked back five scrambled egg whites, a couple of bananas, and a bowl of oatmeal by nine a.m., but I figured I'd likely survive. I watched in silence as she fixed a mug of milk-and-sugar-laden coffee for herself.

"Let's go sit out," she said, and I followed my mother's girlish terry-cloth ass out to the patio. She took a seat at the big round glass-top table, positioning herself under the open umbrella for maximum shade. The sun was as bright as studio lights and I immediately wanted my sunglasses, but rather than going back for them, I resigned myself to squinting and sat down next to Clara. I stared absently at the sunlight shimmering on the surface of the saltwater lap pool and took another sip of the coffee.

A buddy of mine once told me my coffee reminded him of his childhood, when his mother would pour a swig of it and a good deal of sugar into a cup of hot milk for him. She had called it "kettle coffee." I'd never heard the term before and haven't heard it since. He was originally from Canada, so maybe it's a Canadian thing, or maybe his mom just made it up. But milky, sweet coffee always makes me think of Darren. He's dead now. Staph infection. Forty-two years old. Anyway...

I finally turned to Clara, who had also been watching the sunshine on the pool, and asked her, "So, what happens now?"

She turned to face me. "Happens to what?"

"You know, treatment?"

"Oh," she said and shrugged her shoulders (somewhat padded by the bulk of Daniel's robe). "You know, chemo and radiation. Maybe it will shrink the thing. Maybe not." Her face didn't move, her voice was matter-of-fact, as if we were discussing her recipe for okra gumbo. I couldn't help finding it just a bit irritating.

I looked down into my kettle coffee, took a deep breath, and opened my mouth to ask the question that wouldn't seem to leave my throat.

"Two to six months," Clara said. I looked up to find an equivocal little half-smile on her face. "I'm leaving it in the hands of the Lord," she said. I felt the sting of tears at my eyes. All at once, Clara closed her eyes, tilted her head slightly back, and began to sing, her high alto as sweet as the coffee in my mug:

> None but the righteous,
> None but the righteous,
> None but the righteous,
> Shall see God.

She reached over and pressed my hand with hers. I blinked back tears and sang the second verse:

> Take me to the water,

Take me to the water,
Take me to the water,
To be bap-tized.

After breakfast (my mother ate like a fullback: scrambled eggs, toast, and three or four slices of bacon) Daniel made himself scarce— through necessity or by design, I knew not, neither did I give a shit— leaving Clara and me to ourselves for most of Saturday morning and afternoon. We sat at the patio table, reading the desert edition of the *Times* in a silence that was occasionally punctuated by the disapproving tongue-clucking or whispering of "Lord, have mercy" from Clara over some particularly disgusting current event or other. We watched the DVD of *National Lampoon's Christmas Vacation* on Dr and Mrs Weinberger's immense flat-screen LCD monitor (Daniel was fond of pointing out that it was not, repeat, *not* a television but a *monitor*), curled up on the buttery-soft white leather sofa that delineated the family room, holding hands like sweethearts. When I questioned Clara's choice of a Christmas movie in May, she shrugged and said, "May not be here in December."

Chevy Chase was sitting in the attic, wearing his mother's old opera gloves and turban for warmth, watching home movies of Christmases long past, when my mother said, "You seeing anybody?"

I picked up the remote (a contraption only slightly smaller than a two-by-four and which, I believe, controlled every appliance in the entire house) and after some searching, finally found the proper button to pause the DVD: I've never been one for talking during a movie, and this was a subject I wasn't too keen on talking about at all.

"I'm not seeing anyone especially," I said. "I have friends."

"'Friends,'" she repeated flatly.

"I like the rhythm of friendship," I said. "'Here I am, now I'm going.'" It's a line from a 1970s Glenda Jackson movie called *Stevie*. I have several quotes from it that I like to pull out at appropriate moments; they have helped me to create the illusion that I am witty since relatively few people have seen the film.

"You getting laid?" she asked.

"Ma!"

She met my eyes calmly, tilted her head to one side in an unspoken "Well?"

"Yes, Mother Dear," I said. "I make a point of getting my proverbial ashes hauled at least once per week. Okay?"

"And who's hauling these ashes for you?"

"I have lovers," I said. "Not one particular person."

She sniffed her obvious disapproval: "Fuck-buddies."

"Mother, where on earth did you learn that term?"

"*Queer as Folk*," she said.

"Give me strength." I took a deep, cleansing, yoga breath. "Mom, my love life is fine. My sex life is fine. I'd go into detail, but frankly, I'd *so* rather not."

Clara covered the back of my hand with her own small warm palm. "I don't like the idea of you growing old alone," she said.

"Don't look now," I said, "but I already have."

She slapped my hand and said, "*Meshuggeh*! You're barely middle age." She rubbed softly where she'd slapped and said, barely whispering, "It's been fifteen years, baby."

I slipped my hand from under hers. "Fourteen years," I said, perhaps a bit louder than absolutely necessary. "I know exactly how long it's been, thanks very much." Immediately, I felt more than a little ridiculous.

After a moment of unseasonably cool silence, Clara rested her hand on my nearest knee. I allowed it to remain there.

"Forgive me for caring," she said.

"I had a love once," I said, as calmly as I could manage. "A real love. For ten whole years. A lot of people never do, you know. I just don't think I'm going to get another one. Not this lifetime."

I pointed the remote to the screen and pushed "Play."

Chevy fell through the attic door, crashing to the floor, projector and all. Clara laughed softly and said, "That boy sure could fall, couldn't he?"

About five o'clock Saturday afternoon, Clara sent me home. Just like that. We'd just finished our second movie, *A Christmas Story* (she'd laughed so hard during the scene where the little boy's tongue gets stuck to the frozen flagpole, I'd had to pause the movie), when she looked at the delicate gold watch on her wrist and said, "Why don't you go on home now." Dismissed.

"I was sort of planning to spend a few days," I said. I'd already decided to call my boss and ask for at least Monday off.

"There's no point," she said. She looked into my eyes, a little smile on her lips. "I'll be in church most of the day tomorrow and then on Monday ..." she paused, took in a long breath, "I go in for the radiation."

"All the more reason for me to stay," I argued.

She shook her little braid-capped head. "There's nothing for you to be here for."

"I can just *be* there," I said. "I can sit with you and hold your hand, I can—"

"I have a husband for that, baby." One of those double-edged razorblade statements Clara slung now and then. She had a husband for that, and I had none.

45

I said, "Fine, then," and started to push myself up off the couch. Clara took hold of my wrist and pulled me back down, her grip amazingly strong for a tiny lady with a little lump of death nestled against her brain.

"Don't be like that," she said softly. She took my hand in both of hers. "I'll have Daniel call you on Monday, after." She rubbed my hand, as if nursing frostbite. "Why don't you come back and see me in a couple of weeks."

I nearly felt like crying, like a child who'd just been scolded. Or deserted. I didn't understand what she was trying to do; and I told her so.

"I don't want you sitting here, watching me," she replied. "Not for two months and certainly not for six. I want you to go live your life. Go to work, see your friends. Go get yourself loved."

I started to say something, probably nothing worth saying, when she took my face into her hands and kissed me softly on the lips, like a first date. I took her into my arms, small and warm and smelling of Chanel No. 5 (and still just slightly of bacon), and we rocked one another a little while.

I got home at about 7:30. Joni had sung me all the way back. I arrived to Amos and Andy's meow-meow duet, the slightly musty smell of a house that had been closed up for nearly twenty-four hours straight, and three messages blinking on my answering machine. I picked up the phone and called Clara's landline, let the phone ring once, and hung up: our lifelong code for "I made it home in one piece, you can go to sleep now." I let the messages play while scooping out the cat box, which was so full I wondered if the boys had thrown a party while I was gone.

From 10:47 a.m., Saturday: "Hey, Johnnie, it's Jerry." Jerry Wong.

My little Asian power bottom. Sprinter's legs, bulbous buns, and an unsurpassed vocabulary of filthy sex-talk in both English and Cantonese. I felt a tell-tale stirring in my jockeys. "I was hoping you might be free tonight. Call me."

From 2:55 p.m., Saturday: "Hello? You screening your calls, Johnnie?" Rob. This adorable little blond litigator I met at a nude pool party a couple of summers ago. Rob likes to go to trial wearing a steel-grey power suit and contrasting tie, with a jumbo, latex butt plug jammed up his keister. What he likes to do in my Jacuzzi bathtub is nobody's business but our own. "I'm jonesin' bad for you, Johnnie. You free Sunday afternoon? Call me on my cell, anytime." A beat of silence, before he added, "Sir."

From about ten minutes ago: "Hey, Shorty." Dre. "I know you're not coming back 'til tomorrow, but you were on my mind. Didn't want to bother you at your mom's. Anyway, call me when you get home."

"See that, Mom?" I said to myself. "I'm not just getting laid—I'm getting laid by the Rainbow Coalition."

I sat at the computer, opened up Outlook while pushing Dre's number with my free hand. I deleted about a dozen messages out of hand (amazing how much crap gets through the alleged spam-blocker), leaving me two messages from *dudes.com*.

I hadn't been on the site in a couple of months. I'd only signed up in the first place because I'd received a free membership for taking a survey on safer sex practices at LA Pride, and it was about to expire, and why the heck not? A silly screen name ("JohnnieJohnnieJohnnie"), a few uploaded pix (shirtless and smiling, tensing abs and flexing triceps), and of course, stats (forty-eight, five-eight, one-sixty). Homos just *love* numbers. A short list of short answer questions—book: *Just*

Above My Head by James Baldwin; music: Joni Mitchell; movie: *Stage Door* (1937, RKO Studios, Kate Hepburn, Ginger Rogers, Ann Miller, Eve Arden—wise-cracking dame *heaven*); size: big (no brag—just facts); preferred position: top (but I'm not a fanatic about it). Far too many unimaginative messages later—most of them beginning with clever plays on my screen name ("JohnnieJohnnieJohnnie, yummy yummy yummy") and moving swiftly to a confession of undying love for big black dick—it got to be a snore, and as young Ethan likes to say, I dropped it like it's hot.

Dre answered on the third ring.

"Back early," I said. "Can you come over?"

"I'm practically there."

I closed Outlook; later for this shit. Then opened it up again. I double-clicked the first email from *dudes.com*, then double-clicked the link to the message from "Caramel-74." His profile photo was a waist-length snapshot of a boyishly handsome young man with skin the color of, well, caramel. Mixed race, I thought, or maybe Latin, Puerto Rican, or something. Short, dark, and very curly hair, button-ish nose, a smile employing only full lips, no teeth visible. It's hard to tell in pictures, but I would have guessed he was maybe five-foot-seven. He wore a plain white T-shirt full, nearly to bursting, with muscles. Biceps bulged in an upraised arm. He had one hand in his pocket; the other made a peace sign. His message read: "The calla lilies are in bloom again." Kate's signature line from *Stage Door*. I had to smile. Definitely not the same old same old.

I clicked "Respond," typed in Kate's next line ("Such a strange flower, suitable to any occasion"), and then "Email me directly," and my personal email address. It seemed to me that Mr Caramel-74 might turn out to be someone worth meeting up with in meat-space.

Sometime. For now, Dre was coming over, and I needed him (as Kanye said) like Kathie Lee needed Regis.

3.

Dre spent most of Sunday with me, which went a long way toward keeping me from going certifiably batshit crazy. We slept in late— okay, seven or so, which is late for me (the previous morning notwith- standing)—and I breakfasted on his pornographic dancer's ass before getting up, putting coffee on, and scrambling up a mess of eggs. Dre and I sat in bathrobes and socks at opposite ends of my dining table, reading what Dre likes to call the "relevant portions" of the Sunday *Times*: the funnies, the entertainment section, *Parade* magazine, and the sale ads. I was chuckling aloud at *The Boondocks* when Dre nudged my leg with his stocking foot and said, "It's eight-thirty-five, Shorty. We best get ready for church."

This would be a good place for another PowerPoint presentation, title slide: "Johnnie Ray Rousseau's Excellent Spiritual Adventure":

I had been installed as a deacon of my church just three weeks before—see Johnnie in clerical collar, white robe, and gold-embroidered stole, looking (I like to think) rather like Denzel Washington starring in *The Desmond Tutu Story*. That I should even enter a church of my own free will, let alone become a deacon of one, would have seemed unlikely until relatively recently. I had, some thirty years previous, sworn off Christianity in all its myriad forms, largely due to my having been submitted to a "deliverance from unclean spirits" (more or less the evangelical Christian equivalent of exorcism—and, incidentally, my parents' best hope of a miraculous cure for my homosexuality) at the age of seventeen. It is beyond an understatement to say the cure didn't take, and said evangelical exorcism had the effect of turning me against church, all church, any church, for a couple of decades. During which decades I studied Hinduism, Zen Buddhism, *nam-myoho-renge-kyo* Buddhist chanting (like Tina Turner), and Kabbalah (*before* Madonna did it, please note). I consulted palm readers, numerologists, and trans-channelers. Hey, it was the eighties—we did those things. My papa disapproved it, and my mama boo-hooed it; but seeing as they were both convinced that as a practising homosexual, my lumpy lower berth in hell was already bought and paid for, anyhow, the fact that I'd put away the King James Version and picked up the Upanishads, made precious little difference in the price of collard greens at Safeway.

Two semi-related events pointed my feet back toward church. First, I turned forty. With the onset of middle age and the attendant intimations of impending mortality came the desire to go back to church. Just because. And yet, my years of spiritual grazing had brought me not one step closer to deciding what religion, what faith, what discipline (if any) was the true one, the right one. And certainly

Christianity, bastion of homophobia, sexism, and unabashed money-grubbing, wasn't even a contender.

And then, I saw Joseph Campbell on PBS; I had stumbled upon a marathon rerun of the Bill Moyers' *The Power of Myth* series quite by accident, just flipping channels one Sunday afternoon. I paused initially because I was taken aback by the elderly Professor Campbell's rococo facial ugliness—it was a five-car pileup of a talking head, and I couldn't look away. And while I was recovering myself to the point where I could remember what the remote control was for, Campbell said (and if you're taking notes, now's the time), *"All religions are true, as metaphor for something that is unknowable."*

Now, I think the word "epiphany" has been grossly overused of late (as have the words "empower," "self-esteem," and "latte"). So I will simply say that at that moment, I had a great, big *"Ah!"*; a large-scale "Yes!"; and an intellectual and spiritual "Why the hell didn't I think of that?" Already eight years dead at that point, Campbell had expressed in one succinct sentence exactly what I'd suspected since childhood but had never been able to conceptualize, let alone verbalize, to my own satisfaction. And all at once I realized: it didn't freakin' matter *what* church I went to, or temple or synagogue, because no religion was true, and *all* religion was true. Nobody was getting it right: everybody was just making their best guesses. Finally, I decided that the metaphor I grew up with was as good a metaphor as any; so back to Jesus I went, like a repentant backslider at a revival meeting. True, it was something of a long walk—I wouldn't actually set foot in a church for another six years, hand in hand with Dre. He'd spent a typically moist Saturday night at my house, and the next morning, immediately following slightly sour-tasting first-thing-in-the-morning kisses, he said, "Come to church with me."

I hadn't even known Dre *went* to church.

My shoes had hardly touched the worn linoleum floor of the strip-mall storefront that is the First Assembly of Love Church, when a round-faced comb-overed Auntie in a floral-print shirt sidled up and said, "Welcome, Honey!" He asked my name, wrote it onto a large Avery label, and applied it to my shirt just above the left nipple, rubbing my chest a bit longer than was strictly necessary to affix the label securely. Auntie smiled a set of perfect teeth, lifted one silvery eyebrow, and said, "I just *love* this job."

FYI: First Assembly of Love Church in Hollywood is a gay church. There, I've said it. Gay church. It is, in fact, very gay. Gayer than *Queer Eye*. Gayer than Cher tickets and a bottle of silicon-based lube. First Assembly of Love had splintered off of the Metropolitan Community Church sometime in the mid-1980s, long before I ever found it: some dispute over inclusive language or fabric swatches or something. Now, I will admit that during my anti-Christian years, I pooh-poohed the concept of "gay church" pretty much out of hand as the equivalent of an African-American chapter of the KKK. But considering the welcome can be less than warm for obvious queers at mainstream churches, what's an obviously queer Christian to do? Pastor Tom often refers to it as a "refugee church," a term I rather like.

And on the subject of obvious queers, it makes for an amusing exercise to imagine our Pastor Tom—The Reverend Dr Thomas Dodd—behind the pulpit at First Baptist Church of Normal—he of the salt-and-pepper high-and-tight haircut, the meticulous topiary of a goatee, the leather motorcycle pants and steel-toed boots peeking out beneath his white liturgical robe—a leather Daddy in a clerical collar. Our head deacon, Bam (born Bambi, but call her by that name at your own risk) is practically a ten-years-younger, miniature Pastor

Tom: military do, leather pants, boots, everything but the beard. Sam, the boyishly handsome young man at the piano, packs a rolled-up sweat sock in the front of his twenty-eight-waist Calvin Klein briefs, having spent most of his life as a boyishly handsome girl named Cyndi. But at Assembly of Love, they don't (as Tom Petty might say) have to feel like refugees.

Much to my own surprise, I have never felt so at home in church as I have at Assembly of Love. We're small (sixty or so on a good Sunday, largely Caucasian with a few blacks and Latinos, and one lone Asian, a young Korean-American man named Wil, whom I'd love to boink but who doesn't seem to know I breathe). The congregation is about a sixty-forty male-to-female ratio, with (as I've mentioned) a certain amount of blurring in that category. Pastor Tom defines the church as "post-denominational," which I've decided is Latin for "grab-bag." Assembly of Love's congregants come from Roman Catholicism (you'll see the sign of the cross executed in several of the folding chairs serving as pews), Protestantism, Seventh-Day Adventism, and heaven knows what-all. The liturgy strikes me as vaguely Presbyterian and the music tends toward selections from a fairly recent, politically correct hymnal, and various 1960s hippie-dippy love anthems: "Put a Little Love in Your Heart," that sort of thing.

And although I will freely admit to the occasional pang of nostalgia for the gospel-singing, feathered-picture-hat-wearing, gettin'-the-spirit Baptist church of my childhood, such pangs are fleeting, and more than a fair trade for the deep-down feeling of rightness that fills me every time I set foot in Assembly of Love. It is well with my soul. Let the church say Amen.

This particular Sunday, I wasn't on altar duty, nor was I scheduled to sing—young Sam would be soloing "What the World Needs Now Is Love," self-accompanied on piano. So it was easy-go for me. Lilith was ushering, and she handed Dre and me a two-sided bulletin each as we entered. A six-foot-two, rawboned, sixtyish, relatively recent male-to-female transsexual, Lilith (for all her considerable efforts) never fails to remind me of a drag-ball category from the movie *Paris Is Burning*: "Butch queen, first time in drags at a ball." This particular Sunday morning, she was wearing a sherbet-green pantsuit and a pair of matching highheeled sandals that made it necessary for me to go *en pointe* in order to give her a hello kiss on the cheek. "Good morning, darlings," she said in a velvety baritone.

"Do you have the prayer list?" I asked. Lilith retrieved a clipboard from the seat of a nearby chair. "Here it is," she said, handing me the list. "Someone close?"

"My mother," I said.

"I'm so sorry, darling," she said, cupping my face in her hand (a mitt large enough to palm an NBA ball, yet soft and scented and recently manicured). I wrote "Clara Weinberger (Deacon Johnnie's mother)" on the prayer list under the Prayers of Healing and Health category, and returned the clipboard to the chair. Dre's hand was warm at the small of my back as we walked toward the third row of chairs. Little Sam was playing "Jesus Is My Firm Foundation," quietly on the piano. On the iPod in my mind, Clara Weinberger was singing "None but the Righteous Shall See God."

Between staring a hole in my cell phone waiting to hear from Daniel about Clara, and checking and re-checking my personal email hoping for a message from Caramel-74, I wasn't much good to anyone at work on Monday. It would have been easy to have called Harold and told him I wasn't up to it—no explanation would have been necessary—but I'd mistakenly thought coming into the office would make the time pass more quickly. But it wasn't the busiest of Monday mornings, and I whiled away some time perusing Caramel-74's profile on *dudes.com*: his name was Joe (on this website, anyway). Thirty-one years old (*a-ha*, hence the "74"—seventeen years younger than I, said the rusty old abacus in my head). Five foot seven, 170 pounds (quite the little chunk, this one). Book: *The Lion, the Witch and the Wardrobe* (pardon me for living, but I've never read it). Music: DJ BC (which is what? A band? Artist? Genre? Geez, young'uns.). Movie: *Stage Door* (excellent!). Size: average (which, the way men are, might mean "average for a thimble"—not that it much matters to me, mind you). Preferred position: bottom (again, excellent!).

I clicked on the Photo Gallery link, and may well have gasped aloud: if the half-dozen professional-looking color photos spread across my computer screen were anything like a reliable representation, this kid was gorgeous. In T-shirt and jeans, in a square-cut Speedo, in (Mother of Mercy!) red spandex bike shorts—gorgeous! And I don't mean garden-variety West Hollywood works-out-at-least-four-times-a-week gorgeous. I'm talking Colt, Falcon, William Higgins, pre-condom classic porn gorgeous. I shifted my hips around the rapidly growing chub in the crotch of my Gap khakis, then clicked back to Joe's main page to make sure I hadn't stumbled into the Model/Escort section by mistake. Apparently not.

And then I thought, Of course, some Troll has so *totally* posted a bunch of pix of somebody else. Had to be. No actual, real-live, not-a-whore human being looks like that, and if he did, I seriously doubt he'd be posting on *dudes.com* (and not even in Model/Escort), let alone dropping emails to some middle-aged Daddy wannabe. I mean, if you actually look like that, how tough can it be to *meet* people? And, as every urban gay man knows, there is a good forty-percent chance that any man you "meet" on the 'Net will turn out to be (a) significantly (and I mean decades) older than the pictures you saw, (b) several waist sizes larger than the pictures you saw, and/or (c) an entirely different human being than the pictures you saw. I mean, I've known guys to post pix of soap stars, porn stars—heck, I actually once busted a guy using a picture of *me*. It's the 40% Rule. (Just FYI, this is not *my* rule—like an urban legend or a Negro spiritual, the 40% Rule is of unknown origin. But it seems to have been laid down some five minutes immediately following the invention of the Internet.)

I've been burned enough times myself that I've created a stock line for when the muscle stud in the picture turns into the pot-bellied, saggy-boobed Auntie on my doorstep: (Open door.) "Dude, you're totally hot, but my husband just called and he's coming home early. We gotta do this another time." (Close door.)

Yeah, it's a big fat lie. You bait-and-switch me with a self-pic that may or may not have ever been you and I have no moral obligation to be a nice fella. So sue me.

My eye caught the blinking of the tiny MSN Messenger icon at the lower right of my computer screen. Passing my curser over it, I could see by the screenname ("cuteblonddude") that it was Ethan. This was turning out to be a theme morning. Ethan had recently fallen into a long-distance Internet romance with a sixteen-year-old boy in Eugene, Oregon (or at least someone claiming to be a sixteen-year-old boy in Eugene, Oregon). They had yet to meet, either in person or on camera (Ethan's amour claimed to have no web cam, though Ethan did). They had traded JPEGs and voluminous emails, talked rather sparingly on the phone (Ethan's anytime minutes being finite), and chatted online several times a day, every day. (Ethan had shown me Eugene, Oregon's alleged self-pix: a beautiful, vaguely Italianesque young man—rather twenty-something-looking, I thought—with the impressive ab development and slick-looking photography I tend to associate with a professional model. Ethan's pix were charmingly amateurish self-portraits created by pointing his camera-phone at a mirror.)

Ethan had told only me about this little cyber tryst and immediately sworn me to secrecy, knowing full well that neither Maggie nor Sully was likely to take kindly to it. And as often happens when dealing with gay youth, and distractingly beautiful gay youth, in particular (I am ever torn between the desire to be their uncle and the at-least-equal desire to be their Daddy), I went all mommy on Ethan, warning him about the 40% Rule and the danger of trusting anyone he hasn't seen in meat-space. And being a teenager, he ignored me completely. I was the voice of the adult in an old Charlie Brown cartoon—random notes played on a trumpet with a *wa-wa* mute: *wa, wa-wa, wa wa.*

I opened up Messenger. Ethan's message said *Sup?* I typed back, *Allegedly working.*

LOL. I wonder if anyone, in the entire history of the worldwide Web, has ever actually been laughing out loud when they typed LOL? *Im also chatting w Roman.* Roman being the alleged name of Ethan's little cyber squeeze. *He sez it sux u dont believe hes real*, came the next message. And then another, *I told him its cuz u luv me.*

That I do, I typed. He sent me a ☺. I'd told Ethan at least once that I didn't much care for smileys, but apparently that had been just more *wa-wa.*

luv you 2. A beat, and then, *But not like I luv roman.*

I chuckled softly to myself. When I was fifteen, I was the only gay boy I knew, so I squandered my crushes on straight boys. Falling for a cyber-boy was probably no worse. Confident that this little conversation wasn't going to get much more interesting anytime soon, I typed,

Boss at my desk. Later. And signed off of Messenger.

I then checked my Yahoo! account for the fourth or fifth time in as many minutes, to find a fresh email from Caramel-74. Subject line: *I refuse to wash my neck for lamb stew!* Yet another line from *Stage Door.* The message read, *Sup, handsome? I like your pix and profile (particularly your choice of movies—hehehe!). How old are those pix? No way you're 48. Holla back.* It ended with a smiley I wasn't familiar with:

:-P

As I've mentioned, I don't much like smileys, neither am I a huge fan of cutesy-poo e-abbreviations like LOL and IMHO, or emotional indicators like *hehehe.* On the other hand, with that face and that bod, I'd probably forgive uncontrollable flatulence and a severe case of Tourette's. I hit Reply, replaced his subject line with yet another *Stage Door* reference: *Just getting over the DTs.* Then I wrote: *The pix were taken last summer. And while we're on the subject, you expect me to believe those pix are really you?*

I'd hardly hit Send before I got a message back from him: *40% Rule, right? Well, I can prove it. I'm sitting in front of a web cam. See attached.* I scrolled down and clicked on the thumbnail, opening up a three-inch square photo of the very same smokin' hot young man, shirtless and impossibly muscled, smiling and holding up a rectangular glare which I eventually recognized as a piece of paper, on which was written (with a black Sharpie, I'd guess) "Hi Johnnie!"

Apologies, I wrote back. *Couldn't imagine a man hot as you being interested in me. Hard to imagine a man as hot as you, period.*

Seconds later: *Silly man! YOU'RE the hottie. And if you're really 48 and really look that good, I'm sure I'm not the first person who's ever pointed that out.*

Thank you, I typed back. *If you don't mind my asking, what's your ethnicity?*

I had just tapped the Send button when my intercom buzzed. Glancing at the face of my phone, I saw that it was almost ten o'clock. I'd killed nearly an hour and a half without having done a lick of work.

"Johnnie," Harold shouted so loud I could hear him in the phone receiver and also acoustically from his office across the hall from the secretarial bay I shared with a file clerk from Potenza and Dennehy, the litigation firm from which Harold leased office space. "I can't find the Rosenberg file!"

Yes, I am a secretary to an attorney. And as they used to say in the old Warners cartoons, it's a living. Not a big living, mind you, but fortunately I don't need barrels of Benjamins: Keith's life insurance all but paid off the mortgage on the house fourteen years earlier, so like some poor *schmo* sitting on a milk crate at the freeway onramp with a hand-lettered cardboard sign, I pretty much work for food.

As with Maggie and Sully, I met my boss, Harold Benjamin, through Crockett Miller. Harold and Crockett had dated for a while, and remained close buds when the whole sex thing hadn't exactly lit the night skies above LA with fireworks; so over the years I'd shared the occasional dinner, cocktail, and game of Trivial Pursuit with Harold.

Harold had confided to me once that he had promised Crockett that he'd take care of him in sickness. Unfortunately, when Crockett's time did come, Harold was himself hospitalized with AIDS-related pneumonia, so Sully and Maggie and I took over Crockett's care. Harold, of course, recovered. He has been HIV-positive for nearly twenty years now, and remains healthy, physically, anyway.

Crockett's death left Harold with a heaping helping of survivor's guilt and the itch to *contribute* to the gay community rather than just make bushel barrels full of money, so he left the high-profile, high-paying, high-stress entertainment firm he'd been with for years and hung out his shingle as a sole practitioner, specializing in estate planning for gay people. It took Harold several Cosmopolitans and several minutes of stammering to ask me to come work for him (you'd think he was proposing marriage), but as it turned out, my itch to contribute was second only to his. We've been at it now for nearly sixteen years.

"Johnnie, the Rosenberg file!" Harold shrieked into the intercom.

"It's in your office," I said into the phone.

"It's *not* in my office," Harold shouted, not bothering to speak into the phone. I could hear the tell-tale paper shuffling indicating a frantic manual search of his desk.

"Yes, it is," I sing-songed back. "Don't make me have to come in there and find it." My cell phone rang ("Flavor *Flav!*"), punting my vital organs up into my throat. I grabbed my cell, flipped it open, and said, "Daniel, don't go away, I'll be right back." I set the cell down on my desk, got up and hurried into Harold's office, where my boss was doing what I like to call his "early Ed Asner routine": loosened necktie, round face, and shiny bald cranium flushed pomegranate red, scratching at the top of his head with one hand while shoving papers around his desk with the other.

I said, "It's right in front of you, Harold," poking my right index finger on top of a manila file folder in the center of his cluttered desk. He made a noise in his throat that may well have signaled the beginning of an argument, but the subsequent falling of his sloped shoulders and marked diminishing of facial redness signaled his recognition that the file he'd been looking for was, in fact, directly under his arched nose. I said, "My call came," as I left, having warned him early on that I'd be expecting a call regarding my mother's condition.

"I'm sorry, Daniel," I said, sitting down and crouching low behind my computer monitor, silently bemoaning the complete lack of privacy afforded by my cubicle. "Tell me."

"Actually," Daniel said, "the news is pretty good."

"Then she's cured," I said pointedly.

"Of course not, John." The sound of Daniel's voice, deep and raspy, the voice of someone's very worried, extremely tired husband, made me feel like a five-star shitheel for fat-mouthing Daniel at a time like this.

"I'm sorry," I said. "Smart-ass remark retracted."

Daniel chose to ignore. "She's in very good hands, John." He sucked in an audible breath. "Lee Roseman came down from Santa Monica, as a personal favor. He's one of the best oncologists in the country." He quickly added, "An oncologist is a cancer specialist."

"Thank you," I said. "I am, in fact, a complete ignoramus." I just couldn't seem to keep my big yap shut. "I'm sorry," I said, but my foot was pretty much all the way in.

Another big sigh from Daniel. "No, I'm sorry," he said. "I don't always have the luxury of talking with the most educated people. Anyway, Lee—Dr Roseman—he's on the cutting edge of cancer research, including a new series of drugs that are cancer growth inhibitors, such as Iressa. These growth inhibitors can, in some cases, literally starve cancerous tumors to death."

"And Mom's going to have access to these drugs?"

"Yes," he said. "Lee's planning a rather rigorous cocktail, along with the chemo and radiation, for the next eight weeks to start, in the hopes of shrinking the tumor to either a manageable, livable level, or an operable level. So, there is hope."

"Oh my God," I said. I tasted salt and realized I was crying, my forehead against the top of my desk.

Daniel just said, "Yeah"—in a deep sigh, barely recognizable as a word.

"How is she?" I asked, snatching Kleenexes (one, two, three) from the box I always keep on my desk and dabbed at my wet face.

"She's asleep right now. She's pretty tired. The nausea and aching will come later."

"Well, it's always nice to have something to look forward to." I'm pretty sure I could actually hear Daniel's eyes roll.

"Are you always this caustic?" he asked.

"Pretty much," I admitted. "I am a work in progress. Right back," I said, and set the cell phone down to free both hands for a vigorous, flatulent nose-blow. "Beg your pardon," I said into the phone. "I appreciate the call, Daniel. Please keep me posted."

"Of course."

"And I'd like to come visit again, next weekend, if that's okay with you."

"Whenever you want to, John. You know that."

When I'd clicked the phone shut and raised my head, Harold was standing in front of my desk, big furry hands palm-down on the black granite ledge, eyes wide with obvious concern.

He said, "Would you like to take a break?"

I sniffed snot and tears. "If it wouldn't be vastly inconvenient." I quickstepped my way to the men's room (barely avoiding collision with a recklessly driven mail cart along the way), closed myself into a stall, sat down, and had a good, long cry, just on general principles.

When I got back to my desk, there were two emails waiting for me from Caramel-74. The first read: *I'm bi-racial.* Oh, yes: I'd asked. *My mom's black, dad's white. Though I usually just say black—it's faster.*

Think you might want to meet up sometime? The second email said, *You still there?*

I hit Reply: *At work. May I call you this evening? Or you call me.* I added my home and cell numbers, and hit Send.

Almost immediately, I got an email back with a 323 area code with a phone number and, *No land line, just the cell. We'll talk tonight.*

I did manage to get through the work day. I went to the gym from work and, as usual, found that the pectoral pump from a few sets of cable crossovers went a long way toward restoring my relative calm. The bad news was, California Fitness (Centinela Avenue in Santa Monica) on a Monday evening is a freakin' zoo; the good news was, a mob scene at the gym translates into an unusually high level of eye candy—concentrating on the spectacular glutes of a young brother executing a set of toe raises made it just a bit easier to grunt out one last parallel bar dip.

I was home, opening a fourteen-ounce can of chicken breast (to be scattered across a plateful of salad-from-a-bag) for dinner, when the phone rang. I sucked broth off my thumb and answered during the second ring.

"Johnnie, it's Tom." My pastor. Deacon duty, no doubt.

"Wassup, Rev?" Whatever it was, I quietly hoped it would be quick; I didn't have call-waiting (I hate being put on hold and I refuse to inflict such treatment upon others) and I didn't want young Mr Muscles to call and get an earful of busy-signal.

"Peter Wells died this morning," he said. Tom's voice seemed particularly husky. He'd been close friends with Peter, and had likely been crying.

I felt my legs give out beneath me. I sat hard on the linoleum floor, resting my head against the wall beneath the phone. "Shit."

Tom said, "Indeed." He drew an audible breath and continued: "Kevin found him in the shower. Apparently, his heart just gave out."

Peter and Kevin had been together a few years (more than five, fewer than ten, I'd guess). They were among my favorite people at Assembly of Love—both choir members, both cuties, both sweet as could be. Peter had been HIV-positive since the mid-80s, and over the years, had had a case of just about everything—Kaposi's, pnuemocys-titis, a months-long coma, the works—and survived. Like so many poz guys, Peter had in recent years been on testosterone therapy, and he worked out five days a week, so he looked like a god. Leave it to gay men to turn chronic illness into an opportunity to look *fabulous*. And now, Peter was dead—just like that. He was thirty-nine.

Tom said, "Kevin asked if you'll sing at the memorial service."

And I said, "Shit."

"I know," Tom said. "Do you know a song called 'Empty Room'?"

"I don't think so." I beat a Morse code SOS on the kitchen wall with the back of my head.

"Kevin says it's by Marjorie Fair," he said. Never heard of her. "Do you think you could find it, and learn it? By Saturday?"

"I suppose I pretty much have to, don't I?"

"I can always tell Kevin you can't do it," he said, which he and I both knew was not an actual option.

"Any news about your mother?" he asked. I gave Tom the *Reader's Digest* abridged version of that story, thanked him for even remembering to ask (it's just the kind of guy Tom is), and assured him I'd have "Empty Chairs" or whatever the song was, under my belt for the memorial. I pushed myself up from the floor and hung up the phone. The receiver was still in my hand when it rang again.

A smoky, testosterone-heavy voice asked, "Is Johnnie there? This is Joe. Callahan."

"Hey, dude." I pushed at my left pec with my hand—my heart was beating like Krupa. And I *never* say "dude." Easy, Johnnie—he's just a guy.

"Is this a bad time?" he asked. I had the decidedly un-PC thought that the guy didn't sound black—something I'm told constantly and pretty much hate.

I blurted, "My mom's got an inoperable brain tumor and a friend of mine dropped dead in his shower this morning, so one thing and another, I've had better Mondays." I leaned forward, resting my forehead against the wall, and added, "And how are all *your* folks?"

I heard a deep-throated chortle followed by, "God, I'm so sorry. It's just that, you quoted *Stage Door*." I had to laugh myself.

"I did, didn't I?"

"Man," he said after a moment, "I'm really sorry."

"No, I'm sorry," I said. "You didn't sign up for that."

"Do you want to do this another time?" he asked.

"Do what?"

"Well, I was hoping to make a date. You know? Meet you?"

"Even though I am obviously falling apart?" I wasn't too sure what kind of company I would be—that night, the following night, or any night in the foreseeable future—but the thought of connecting with Joe Callahan in the flesh went some distance toward lifting what I could tell was the beginning of a blue-ribbon depression.

"Even though," he said. "If you're cute as your pix, I don't care if you drool." And then he quickly added, "You don't drool, do you?"

"Not since they adjusted the meds," I said. "You wanna maybe meet for a drink, say, tomorrow?"

"I just got cast in a play," he said. "First read-through tomorrow night, and then rehearsals through Friday. How about Saturday? Dinner, eight-ish."

"I'm very fond of dinner," I said (unable to resist yet another *Stage Door* reference), "but I can't. I've got this gig. I'm a singer. But it should be over by nine or so. How about after?"

"Can't," he said. "I've got to be somewhere at eleven."

"Hot date?" I asked, and immediately cringed. I knew good and well that it was none of my beeswax, but the question had just slipped out.

"No," he said—I'm pretty sure I detected a tolerant little chuckle in there. "Definitely not a date. It's sort of a gig, too."

"An acting thing?"

"Not exactly," he said. And I thought, okay—he doesn't want to tell you. Let it go, Johnnie, let it go. I was about to suggest maybe we *should* just let it go, when Joe said, "Could I come and hear you sing? It wouldn't be a real date, but at least we could meet in, you know, meat-space."

"Um … yeah. Sure."

"Sure?" he said.

"Sure I'm sure. May I come to your, whatever the thing is, after?"

"No," he said quickly and maybe a bit too loudly. "I mean, it's not … um … public."

"Okay," I said, not entirely sure how okay it really was. "I'll put you on the list, then. It's at the Comedy Corral, on Sunset. I'm opening for a friend of mine who's a standup. I'll go on about eight."

"Perfect," he said.

"Perfect," I parroted, for no good reason. "See you then."

"Later, then."

Hanging up the receiver, I could feel the corners of my lips lifting. There was definitely something about this Joe Callahan person.

4.

The week blurred by, as weeks do. I went to the office and expertly shifted paper from one side of my desk to the other—a living tribute to the relative uselessness of a university education (and a BA in English, in particular). During a Tuesday afternoon lull, I Googled Marjorie Fair—turned out Marjorie Fair was a band, not a person—then went to my favorite online music store (*musicnotes.com*), bought a digital copy of the sheet music to the song, printed it out, scanned it, and emailed a PDF copy to little Sam, who'd be playing piano for me at Peter's memorial service. That evening, I downloaded the record from iTunes—a nice enough rock ballad, and appropriately dirge-like. I swear, if I wasn't a Christian, I'd be a priestess at the Temple of the Internet. (A very Auntie thing to say, but there you go.)

I called Clara's house on Tuesday, and then again on Wednesday—

both days around noon, which seemed a relatively safe time: not too early, not too late. Both times, I got Daniel, who told me Clara was sleeping.

"She's weak and tired," he explained on the Tuesday call. "She's not keeping any food down." After a moment, he added, "This will get better." Both times, I asked him to tell my mother I'd called and both times he said he would. Then, Thursday evening, Daniel called me; in the middle of *Will & Grace*, for cryin' out loud, it wasn't a great episode, but still.

"Clara asked me to call," he said. This couldn't be good. I'm not sure if you can actually feel your blood pressure rise, but I'm pretty sure I did. "I know you were planning to come down this weekend," Daniel continued. "Clara asks that you don't."

"What are you talking about?" I sat up rigid, my body flushed with adrenaline. I could have tossed a Toyota.

"She doesn't want you to see her like this."

"She's my *mother*!" I protested.

And Daniel said, "I know, John. And she's my wife. And my wife has asked me to ask you to give her a week or two."

I sucked in enough breath for the sentence I was thinking, that the whole point here was that my mother might not *have* a week or two. But I let it go. I liked to think I did have some vague sense of how difficult this all was for Daniel. I'd been somebody's husband once.

I said, "Tell her I love her."

Beat.

"I will, John."

The phone rang again during the *Will & Grace* end credits.

"Is this the Beacon Laundry?" It was Joe and his dark chocolate voice and yet another in our ongoing series of *Stage Door* references. I smiled in spite of everything.

We'd been trading an average of four emails a day, all week. Just small talk: what music do you like (he doesn't like Joni, but loves Mariah—whom I cannot abide—but we agreed on Billie); favorite movies (in addition to *Stage Door*, we both dug *The Matrix* and *Trick*, but he loved *Crash*, which I pretty much hated). Joe had told me a little bit about the play he'd had been cast in: a fifty-seat theater in Hollywood; he was playing a young man who seduces an entire family—husband, wife, and teenage son. (I didn't have the heart to tell him Michael York had done that dance in *Something For Everyone* back in the 70s.) He'd confessed to having the letch for the director, a forty-ish Korean with a heavy accent and a wife.

"No, it's the Footlights Club," I said, continuing the movie quotes.

"Are you sure?"

"Of *course*, I'm sure—I'm standin' right *in* it!"

I was pretty sure I could actually hear Joe smile. "Notice I waited until after *Will & Grace*," he said.

"A wise young man, indeed."

"Everything okay? Is this a bad time?"

"No, this is fine. Why do you ask?"

"Nothing," he said. "It's just—look, I realize I don't know you, but you sound like," and I heard him chuckle, "light and sophisticated, but inside your heart is breaking." Yet another *Stage Door* reference, but he pretty much nailed me. "Is it your mom?" he asked.

I fell back into the sofa. "I don't want to bore you with my personal shit."

Joe said, "Bore me."

So I gave him the radio edit of my conversation with Daniel. At the fadeout, Joe said, "Sucks. Wish I was there to give you a hug."

"Maybe Saturday?" I said.

And he said, "Count on it."

Friday evening, I sang another chorus of the Mama Won't See Me Blues for the Sullivans, over fried-meat fondue.

"Totally blows," Ethan said, massaging my left trapezius muscle with the long fingers of his right hand.

"Thanks, Buddy," I said, shaking the excess oil off the square of sizzling brown sirloin on the end of my fondue fork, "it does indeed blow." I looked at Ethan with what I hoped was a passable smile. Ethan smiled back, a Botticelli angel in a Coldplay T-shirt.

"Give her time," Maggie said, biting the fat end off of a jumbo shrimp, "severely ill people can require a lot of patience. I remember how it was with Crockett."

"She's right," Sully said, skewering three cubes of raw steak.

I nodded, chewing a mouthful of beef with particular thoroughness to avoid answering back to Maggie and Sully that I already knew what severely ill people could require, having dealt with considerably more severely ill people than either of them had over the past quarter century or so.

One thing and another, I wasn't feeling particularly chatty that night. I didn't even mention that I'd be spending Saturday morning at a friend's funeral. I didn't talk about Joe Callahan, either, though, of course, there would have been little to say, considering we hadn't actually met yet. Fortunately, our inevitable Dominoes game required little conversation other than light trash talk. Ethan and I annihilated his parents two games out of three, after which I excused myself. Sully and Maggie served me appropriately encouraging noises with their goodnight hugs. Ethan hugged me hard—I heard my vertebrae pop. He leaned in close and whispered, "Love you." I managed "Love you too" with what little breath he'd left me.

I hate singing at funerals. Especially if it's for someone I know and even halfway care about. Funerals and memorial services are a time for those of us left behind in this vale of tears, to grieve and mourn and wail and, one hopes, grab a handful of closure. None of which is likely to occur if you're there to *perform*.

I had liked Peter Wells quite a lot. We'd sat together in the tenor section of the choir. We'd traded recipes and ribald jokes and tips for working the long belly of the triceps. As I may have already mentioned, he'd been one of my favorite people at Assembly of Love. But on Saturday morning, as steroid-muscled men in full leather and their cowboy-costumed boyfriends wept like little girls, I sat dry-eyed in row one, in black dress pants and a tasteful but flattering grey shirt. Dre sat next to me, but didn't touch me, knowing me well enough to surmise that physical contact would be of no help. Across the sanctuary, the widowed Kevin sat next to Pastor Tom, wearing his favorite authentic-to-the-last-detail LAPD uniform, tucked under Tom's beefy arm, both of them watering their mustaches with tears. But I didn't have that luxury: I had a show to do.

Which meant that some time later, a week, a month, maybe more—I'd be blindsided by the grief I was currently forced to swallow back, like a throatful of bile: I'd be at the office taking a phone message for Harold, or watching a movie on DVD, or a song would pop up on my iPod in shuffle mode, and, suddenly, I'd be crying myself hoarse. This I knew from experience. I'd been there.

I followed the program sitting on my lap until the appointed time, then crossed to the front of the church and perched on a stool behind a black steel music stand that held the sheet music for "Empty Room." Normally, I'd rather have a prolonged nosebleed than perform while reading the music—but try as I might, I hadn't been able to commit the song sufficiently to memory, to feel comfortable singing it without the sheet. In my twenties, I could hear a song on the radio in the morning, have it memorized by mid-afternoon, and work it into my cabaret act that night. Ah, mid-life.

I nodded to Sam (who had slicked his dirty-blond hair back with a fistful of product and looked very David Bowie Thin White Duke period) and he hit the intro. I gripped the mic stand with both hands and sang,

> I don't wanna go, but if I die young
> Fill my empty room with the sun...

Kevin hummed a throaty continuo, a sound of grief and love lost, yet remarkably in harmony.

I would have hugged Kevin afterward, but the crowd of cowboys, leather folk, and uniforms was thick around him (a cattle call of Village People understudies), so I kissed Dre a quick goodbye, tucked my sheet music under my arm, and left. I needed to get home: I had another gig that night.

Now, there may be uglier places for a black, queer, jazz-influenced pop singer to play than a comedy club in Hollywood, but I can't imagine where (except maybe opening for some thrash band with high-volume hair and a name like "Severe Tire Damage" at the Troubadour). I had only agreed to do this one little twenty-minute set at the Comedy Corral as a big, fat personal favor to Robert Franks, who's a standup comic. Gay, but *deep* in the closet—I mean the smell of moth balls precedes him. He's also a buddy of mine (okay, we also tricked once, it was not pretty, we will not go into it here).

Robert was putting together an industry showcase at the Comedy Corral and needed an opening act. Now, the last thing a standup wants as the opening act for an industry showcase is another standup comic. It's like, *Mother of God, what if he's funnier than I am?* Which pretty much leaves singers, dog acts, and those guys who spin plates on sticks. Robert, Lord love him, had once been instrumental in getting me a relatively decent gig at a relatively decent jazz club in Redondo Beach, and he decided to call in the favor. Which is how I found myself onstage at the Comedy Corral, wearing my basic stage uniform (black Calvin T-shirt, black jeans, black loafers), crooning a few of the quirkier numbers from my long-ago cabaret repertoire, accompanied by the house pianist, a slender young fellow with an Adam's apple the size of a walnut, and an amazing inability to keep a steady rhythm.

As comedy club audiences go, this one was better than average—at least half of them actually acknowledged my existence, and some of them even seemed to acknowledge that I was singing. True, I had tailored a set all but devoid of jazz sensibility and unusually high in novelty material. It was definitely not a Gershwin-followed-by-Cole-Porter kind of evening. So, I pulled out an old ribald blues tune called "You've Gotta Give Me Some" by Bessie Smith and "The Penis Song" from *Monty Python's The Meaning of Life*. No scat breaks, no ballads, no "Moody's Mood for Love," just wham, bam, gee-thanks-you've-been-great, and I'm outta there.

So, I'm smack in the middle of "Come to the Supermarket (in Old Peking)" (which I'd stolen from Barbra's first album, and which had been a staple of my cabaret set back when God was a little girl), when I suddenly noticed this hunky little man-muffin who I'm pretty sure is Joe Callahan, perched on a stool at the bar, which is way in the back, behind the tables. I hadn't seen him come in; and truth to tell, I actually hadn't given him a moment's thought for the half-hour/forty-five minutes leading up to walking onstage. That's just my way: if I've got a gig, that's all I'm thinking about. So suddenly, there he was. And even with the house lights down and a follow spot bearing down on my face, I could tell he was even cuter than his pictures. And he was smiling one of the widest, toothiest, most incandescent smiles ever to light up a small and rather humid roomful of slightly drunken humanity.

Generally speaking, it is not a particularly good idea to focus on the attractive lips, teeth, and gums of an audience member while performing a fast-paced, wordy patter song, as one is apt to lose one's place—which is exactly what I did, somewhere in the middle of the third verse. So I stopped, and just sort of stood there in the middle of the stage for what must have seemed an inordinately long time, while the pianist boom-chicked for about sixteen bars before finally giving up.

And then I laughed. Laughed a good, long coyote barking laugh, staggering back a couple of paces, and then stepped back to the mic, as the audience laughed with me and/or at me.

I did a big, vaudevillian shoulder shrug and said, "So sue me, already." Glancing across the room, I made eye contact with Joe. Our grins met over the heads of a couple near the center of the room.

I counted off a loud "five, six, seven, eight" toward the pianist, and finished the number to loud laughter and even louder applause. America loves a comeback.

I closed the set with "Lydia the Tattooed Lady," which has never been known to fail, and what's-his-name played me offstage to a round of applause that likely struck terror into dear Robert's heart—I mean, one would prefer one's warm-up act to warm the audience up, but one generally doesn't want one's warm-up act to *kill*.

I made a quickstepping beeline to the rear of the room, where—God is good—there was a conveniently vacant barstool right next to Joe, who, I discovered upon approaching, was even better looking up-close than from across the room. He looked like one of those Tom of Finland dolls they sell at The Pleasure Chest, somewhat shy of full-size and somehow brought to life. He greeted my arrival by tossing me that smile of his and saying, "You're wonderful." And, damned if he wouldn't have had me on the speaking voice alone. Even better in person than on the phone.

"Thank you," I said, grinning like the Cheshire Cat on Ecstasy, "very much." I motioned to the empty stool and said, "May I?"

"Please," he said, and I sat beside him. "So we meet at last," he said, offering a smallish, square-fingered right hand, which I readily accepted.

"It is a decided pleasure," I said.

"The pleasure's mine. You were wonderful," he added, our hands still clasped. "I said that already, didn't I?"

"I'm cool with that," I said, finally relinquishing Joe's hand.

Joe turned to the bartender (a tall, brick-muscled fellow with a rapidly receding hairline and a handlebar mustache) and lifted an empty Calistoga bottle. "Another, please." Then to me, "May I buy you a drink?"

"You may," I said. "The same," I said to the bartender, and back to Joe, "Thanks."

We clinked our little bottles together, toasting nothing specific. I couldn't stop grinning, or staring at Joe: his key-lime eyes, his edible-looking toast-brown skin (entirely too much of which was hidden beneath a white microfiber T-shirt and a pair of stretch jeans), and Mother Macree, that smile.

"Damn, you look good," I said. I didn't mean to verbalize it, but suddenly there it was.

"So do you," he said. And then we grinned some more. Finally, Joe said, "I was already on the guest list for this show. I'd forgotten about it."

"You know Robert?" I asked. And suddenly I thought, Shit—is this guy Robert's boyfriend? "Are you—?" I began.

"Oh, no," Joe cut me off. "We're just friends."

"Good," I said. "I mean—" Well, there was no graceful way out of that one, so I just shrugged and said, "I guess I mean, 'good.'" Which earned me another smile. I quickly found Joe Callahan's smiles to be dangerously habit forming. I was already jonesin' for my next fix.

The emcee came onstage to introduce "a very funny guy—ladies and gentlemen, Robert Franks!"

I joined in the applause for Robert's entrance, shouted "Go 'head, Robert," and for the ensuing forty-some-odd minutes, I did my best to focus my attention on Robert's set. I knew most of his material already, which was generally amusing if not spectacularly original, covering the usual sort of late Baby Boomer comedy subjects: dating (and I mean male/female dating, thank you very much), old television shows ("Didn't you ever wonder about Gilligan and the Skipper? I mean, really!"), people who bring eleven items to the ten-items-or-less checkout—that sort of thing.

But try as I might to pay attention to the man on stage (and I promise you, I did try), I spent the duration of Robert's showcase set preoccupied—nay, utterly consumed—by the young man seated next to me. Sensing the heat of his big-muscled arm near mine; enjoying the way his pumped-up pecs and perky nipples pushed out against the microfiber; warming myself in the glow of that smile; and sporting an incessant boner as I imagined wham-bamming Joe Callahan in every room of my house, my back yard, my front yard, and the fully-reclining passenger seat of my Honda.

And then Robert said, "Thanks, you've been great, I mean it, good night," and again I joined the applause as Robert took one, then another shallow bow from the waist, blew a kiss off his fingertips, and left the stage. As the house lights came up and chairs scraped against the floor, I turned to Joe and said, "I'm glad you came."

"So am I," he said, sliding down from the barstool. "I'd better get going. I've got this thing I've got to go to."

"So you've said."

"I'd love to blow it off," Joe said, touching my arm lightly with fingertips that seemed to paint my skin with goosebumps, "but I really can't. What's your schedule like tomorrow?"

"Free," I said, a smile returning to my lips. "I'm totally free tomorrow. Well, after twelve, anyway. Church."

Joe smiled (turning my ankles into bread pudding) and said, "Great. Call me tomorrow, after church."

"Okie-doke," I said, which (I swear to God) is not an expression I use. For some reason, powerful attraction to a man tends to produce something very like dementia in me.

"Where're you parked?" Joe asked.

I stood at the curb, side by side with Joe Callahan, waiting for one of a crew of small, killer-handsome young Latinos in ill-fitting black pants and too-short neckties to return with my car from wherever it is valet parking guys leave five-year-old Hondas. Joe stood close enough for me to smell his cologne (I couldn't place it, but I liked it—he smelled rather like a freshly baked cookie). Close enough for me to brush the back of my right hand softly against the back of his left, which made my crotch swell like a lump of bread dough in a warm kitchen. (What was it about Joe that made me think of baked goods?)

"So what did you say this gig of yours is, that you have to go to at this ungodly hour?" I asked.

Joe glanced at his wristwatch. "It's nine-twenty," he said. "Not as ungodly as all of that." After a moment, he added, "I didn't say. Fact is, I dance."

"I should have guessed," I said. "You have a dancer's ass."

"So do you," he said.

"Actually," I said, leaning in toward Joe, "I have what a buddy of mine likes to call a B.B.B."

"Black boy butt," we said in stereo.

Joe laughed that deep husky laugh that matched his sexy voice so perfectly. "Well, I half-qualify for that, don't I?" he said.

I was thinking up a bright remark when I felt a touch at my shoulder. A nice-looking thirty-something blonde in an expensive-looking black strapless and fuck-me pumps, towing her nice-looking thirty-something date by the hand, paused just long enough to say, "Really enjoyed your singing."

"Thank you," I called toward the two retreating backs. "Thanks very much."

"I'll tell you all about it tomorrow, okay?"

At which point, a short, handsome stranger drove up in my car.

"This is me," I said. I extended my right hand to Joe. He caught me up in a hug, to my breath-catching surprise, and the sudden, full-body contact (the muscle-and-bone force of his bodybuilder arms, his edible-sweet scent, his crisp hair against my face) was almost more than I could take without my legs giving out.

"I owed you a hug," he said as he released me, weakened nearly to the point of collapsing against him. "Remember?"

I managed to draw in enough breath to say, "Thank you."

"Call me tomorrow," he said. Then he took a half step toward me, smiled a wide one, and said (so softly I nearly had to lipread), "I promise—I'll be worth the wait."

I smiled back. "Like Janet?"

He nodded. Gorgeous, and he even gets my semi-obscure Janet Jackson reference.

The valet swung my driver's side door open so wide I feared a passing vehicle speeding toward Beverly Hills might wrench it free. I tipped the little guy a five (I was feeling pretty darn good), slid into the driver's seat and executed the finger-wiggling wave I'd stolen from Liza in *Cabaret* as I left Joe Callahan, his stretch-denim dancer's ass and (Lord have mercy) that smile, curbside in front of the Comedy Corral.

Heading west on Santa Monica, I suddenly (and for no good reason) decided to stop at Circus of Books to pick up the latest *GQ* (Brad Pitt was on the cover). I pulled into the twenty-four-hour-monitored, quarters-only metered parking lot across the street from the store, which (since it was Saturday night and the lot not only faces the book store but backs up onto the Gold Coast, a friendly neighborhood beer, pool table, and heavy-cruise bar), was completely full. In a rare stroke of luck, someone was pulling out of a space, and I pulled in.

I walked through the lot, passing a man leaning into the driver's side window of a parked car making hushed conversation with the man inside; a husky, very black man leaning against another car wearing only a pair of sneakers and some spandex shorts that clearly outlined a set of genitals that would not have seemed out of place on a bison; and a pair of healthy young specimens in jeans and no shirts, engaged in a public show of affection against the hood of yet another automobile. The smell of booze and sweat and the sounds of clinking glass, bar talk, and the bass-heavy boom-de-boom of "Pon de Replay" by Rihanna, poured from the open front door of the Gold Coast as I crossed the street.

Entering the bookstore, I paused in the doorway, my eyes blinking against the sudden brightness of the room. On my way to the magazine racks, I nearly tripped over a wire bin filled with back issues of various gay men's magazines. Looking down, my eyes immediately fell upon the cover of a nearly decade-old issue of *In Touch for Men*, from which smiled a handsome, shirtless young man bearing a resemblance to Joe Callahan far too striking to be mere coincidence.

I opened the mag, flipped pages until I reached the photo layout entitled, "Joey Lee Turner—Bubblin' Brown Sugar." Six pages of photographs (including the centerfold) depicted a visibly younger, slightly less muscular, and gloriously naked Joe: sprawled in an over-stuffed leather chair, legs spread wide, plump hard-on nestled against corrugated belly; sitting cross-legged on a cushion, pinching his own milk chocolate nipples; and on all fours on somebody's bed, the deep valley of his dancer's ass cleverly coinciding with the page fold of the magazine. My dick swelled to uncomfortable dimensions in my jeans. I closed the magazine and pictured President Bush on the john, grunting out a big one, which proved an effective soft-on.

I walked to the front of the store and slapped the magazine onto the counter. The young Latino clerk looked like a pornographer's rendering of Cochise: black straight hair down to the shoulders, cheekbones to kill. His tighty-tight, sleeveless faded-denim shirt was open to the navel, revealing pectoral cleavage and abdominal muscle separation remarkable even by West Hollywood standards. He glanced at me with heavy-lidded black eyes, then looked down at the magazine and said, "Well, look at Joe."

"You know him?" I asked.

"Know her?" he replied in a voice considerably higher pitched than I'd expected. "*Had* her."

The immediate twinge of envy I felt was just that—a twinge, nothing more. That's my story and I'm sticking to it.

I paid for the magazine with my debit card, and was out the door and halfway to the car before I realized I forgot to buy *GQ*.

Church the next morning was on the surreal side. For one thing—centering prayer notwithstanding—I was severely scattered. I had Joe Callahan (a.k.a. Joey Lee Turner) on the brain. I'd taken the magazine to bed with me and between oil-based lube and a voluminous money-shot across a couple pages, I'd pretty much ruined it. I didn't dream about Joe (or anything else I could recall), but his butterscotch booty was my very first mental image upon awakening. A triple-X slide show played behind my eyes as I showered (and yes, jerked off again), made and ate breakfast, and drove to church.

Fortunately, I had no solos to sing, and I couldn't have said for sure whether Pastor Tom preached a sermon or rode a pogo stick. Behind the altar, I spoke the communion liturgy absently, reading my lines like some has-been actor in a fifth-rate road company, with one eye on the wall clock across the room. It was a low Sunday (which is church talk for more empty chairs than usual), so communion promised to be relatively quick. Sam's rather ham-fisted rendering of "I Come to the Garden Alone" provided the soundtrack as worshippers filed up (one by one, in couples, in groups) to the altar to munch a communion wafer dunked into a stainless-steel chalice of grape juice (the intinction method of partaking of the elements—or the "chip and dip" method, as Bam liked to call it), and then to Tom, Bam, or myself for a brief prayer of blessing; all of which was making for a sort of white noise to accompany the "*Joe Callahan Show*" playing in my brain. I shook my head in a thoroughly vain attempt to clear it—I mean *enough*, already—when a man I didn't recognize approached me for a blessing.

I didn't recall ever seeing him before; he may have been introduced as a first-time visitor at the beginning of service, but I couldn't have said for sure. If asked, I probably would have described him as an older man, but he was probably only in his fifties (that is, just a bit older than me). His face was drawn and his hair lank, greasy, and of indeterminate color. A grey T-shirt (at least I hoped it had always been gray) hung from his bony shoulders. He smelled like a five-foot stack of overflowing ashtrays. The man made the sign of the cross, then reached up and grasped my shoulders with very dirty and surprisingly strong fingers.

"Father," he said, his breath so pungent my eyes watered, "I need forgiveness."

My mind had barely processed the fact that he'd called me "Father" before he continued: "I'm schizophrenic, I'm a homosexual, I'm NAMBLA," he said. "I'm a sinner," he added, his fingers squeezing my shoulders hard. He released my shoulders and said, "Forgive me," as he lowered to his knees. He took my hands in his, bowing his head low.

FYI: no matter how preoccupied you might be, a demand for absolution from an admitted schizophrenic boy-lover will very likely snap you right out of it. I could feel my heart rate kick up a notch. I gulped a big breath.

"Please, get up," I whispered, tugging the man up by the hands. He held my hands so tightly it made my fingers ache.

He stared into my face with red-rimmed eyes brimming with tears.

"Forgive me," he repeated. He blinked, and tears fell, settling into the various creases along his cheeks. I've never been much good with crying people. My immediate reaction is to cry with them.

"What's your name?"

He sniffed a wet one and said, "George."

"George," I repeated, and brought his hands to my chest. I searched the ceiling for appropriate words. Finally, I managed, "God forgives." I'd meant to explain somehow that I, of all people, was in no position to forgive anyone of anything, that this was God's job. But what came out of my mouth was "God forgives." And all at once I was talking— and I must admit, if I had been the proverbial fly on the wall, I would likely have thought the small black man in the long white dress was speaking with some authority; though frankly, I didn't much know what I was talking about or where what I was talking about was coming from. "Your mental illness is no sin," I said. "And certainly your homosexuality is no sin." I stopped short at the thought of the whole boy-love thing. I mean, I had no way of knowing if Brother George actually boinked little boys, or just really, really *wanted* to boink them, or just looked at pictures, or what. So I decided to let that one ride for the time being. George just looked at me, tears puddling in his sunken eyes.

I shut my eyes tight and prayed, "God of Love, You hear our prayers before we give them voice; You forgive us even before we ask. Bless my brother George this morning. Where there is sickness of body, mind, or spirit, lift it from him, if it be within Your will. Fill him with life and light. This I ask in the name of Jesus Christ, Amen."

When I opened my eyes, George was smiling, his teeth as brown as my hands. Tears tumbled down his face again.

"Thank you, Father," he said and, taking me by the shoulders again, he leaned in and kissed me on the lips. And while I have never actually licked an ashtray, I would imagine the overall effect would be remarkably similar.

George had hardly turned and begun his shuffling way back to his seat before my head began to throb as if an anvil had been dropped on me from the ceiling: I actually saw stars. The room tilted and I felt my breakfast working its way upward. Someone (I couldn't have said who: my vision was beginning to swim) started toward me, but I whispered an "excuse me" through clenched jaws and hurried down the center aisle and out the swinging doors toward the unisex, wheelchair-accessible restroom. I made my genuflection to the porcelain font just in time.

I walked into the open door of Pastor Tom's office on legs still a bit unsteady. Tom was muscling the heavy wooden hanger holding his hooded robe into the overstuffed closet housing the pastoral drag, altar dressings, and other tools of the trade.

"You feeling all right, Johnnie?" he said. "I was worried."

"Might I have a moment of your time?" I asked, pulling my white satin liturgical stole over my head. I ripped open the Velcro fastenings of my robe and hung it over my arm.

Tom said, "Of course," and I closed the door shut behind me and pushed in the doorknob lock with my thumb.

"Sit," he said, lowering his considerable heft into a chair. I sat opposite him. "Problem?" he asked.

"Somebody confessed to me," I said. "Crossed himself, called me 'Father,' and freakin' confessed."

Tom chuckled. "That'll happen," he said, and gave me a palsy-walsy little pat on the knee. "You're wearing the collar now. Don't let it throw ya."

"But one of the things he confessed—" I began, but Tom cut me off.

"No," he said firmly, pointing a thick index finger in my direction as if ordering a puppy off of the white sofa. "You can't tell me. Whatever it is, that's between you and him. It's a little thing called 'clergy confidentiality.'"

I opened my mouth to speak, but didn't. Then reconsidered and said, "What if it's illegal?"

"Was it?" he asked.

"I don't know," I admitted.

Now it was Tom's turn to open a speechless mouth. He lifted that finger again, then dropped his hand to his thigh, and looked away. After a bit, he looked back at me and asked, "He hasn't killed anybody, has he?" I shook my head no. "Beat somebody up?" No. "Then I think you should keep it to yourself." Tom reached over and took my right hand in both of his (which were as huge and leathery as little-league baseball gloves).

"I know this can be difficult sometimes, Johnnie," he said, massaging my hand with his big thumbs. I looked up into his smallish, hazel eyes. "But it comes with the territory. People have to be able to tell their clergy anything." Tom let go of my hand and repeated, "Anything." He smiled that sexy, slightly lopsided smile of his. "Okay?" I nodded. "Good."

I briefly considered asking if sudden nausea came with the territory, but I let it go and stood up. "Thanks, Tom," I said through a smile I didn't quite believe.

I was pulling out of the church parking lot when my cell phone rang (the tinkle-tinkle-tink of Samantha's nose twitch from *Bewitched*, my generic ringtone).

"Wha's up, Daddy?" said a husky, instantly familiar voice—and yes, I totally wallowed in hearing him call me Daddy. I grinned so wide so fast, I nearly pulled a cheek muscle. I drove back into the parking space; I hate it when people talk on the phone while driving and I try not to do it myself.

I said, "Joe," as if it were a complete thought.

"So, were you gonna call me, or what?" he said.

"I was just about to," I said. "I'm just leaving church."

"So what you got going the rest of today?"

"Jack nothin'," I said. "I'm free from here on out."

"Great," Joe said. "Your place or mine?"

"You're in Hollywood, right?"

"West Hollywood."

"I live in Mar Vista," I said. "So it makes more sense for me to come to your place, if that's okay."

"Just make it quick, Daddy," he said.

Joe Callahan lived in perhaps the smallest apartment I'd ever seen outside of New York City—a single with kitchenette. You could have fit the entire apartment into my master bedroom walk-in closet and still have room for all my shoes. There was a single bed covered with a light-blue chenille bedspread against the far wall and a small grey-painted metal desk (with matching wheeled secretarial chair), probably salvaged from some old, closed bank, on which perched a Mac computer flanked by a pair of outsized speakers. And that was about it.

Except for the angels.

The entire place was full of angels.

A flock of baby-faced, birdy-winged cherubs in every medium, from terracotta and glazed ceramic to various woods, papier-mâché, molded plastic, and construction paper cut-outs, circled the room just below ceiling level, nailed, thumbtacked, or Scotch-taped to walls in some need of paint, walls decorated well past the point of clutter with postcards, Christmas cards, and magazine clippings of winged ones. A battalion of angel Christmas-tree toppers stood in formation atop the chest-high semi-wall separating the kitchenette from the rest of the apartment. A framed poster of the Broadway production of *Angels in America* hung above the bed. A poster of a pointedly homoerotic angel (a beautiful reclining naked boy with superimposed wings, with some sort of makeup or body paint highlighting his lips, pecs, and fat, tumescent penis), a picture I remembered from a coffee-table book on male nude photography, and which I now recognized as a picture of Joe), hung on the wall over the computer.

I stood in the doorway, and took in the room.

"So I guess it's safe to assume that you're into angels," I said. "Me too."

"Honestly?" Joe said, shutting the door behind us.

"Not quite to this degree," I said. "But I've always had a thing about them." My own fascination with angels is largely musical: "Guardian Angel" by Jane Wiedlin, "Angel of Mine" by Monica, "Yes, I'm Your Angel" by Yoko Ono, that kind of thing. I have scads of angel songs stored in my iTunes. I made a quick mental note to burn a compilation CD of angel songs for Joe.

"Angels are all around us," Joe said, turning to face me. "They watch over us, take care of us." He encircled my waist with his arms. I hung my arms over his shoulders. "I wanted to express that visually," Joe said, just before our mouths met. We kissed a warm, wet, sloppy little mess, Joe's mouth tasting so sweet to mine that I smiled as I kissed. A little sound of satisfaction erupted in my throat and escaped from between my lips, and I passed it to Joe from the tip of my tongue to the tip of his, just before he leaned his face away from mine.

"There's something I need to tell you," Joe said, suddenly serious.

"Are you sure you want to talk now?" We stood with arms around each other's waists, the lump of my hard crotch pressed against the equally hard lump of his.

"It's important," Joe said.

"All right," I said, and licked a squiggly little stripe up the bridge of Joe's nose. "Talk."

"Well," he began, "the gig I had last night. I was go-go dancing at a circuit party in Hollywood. It was a favor for a friend. I don't really do it that much anymore." He smiled. "I'm getting kind of old for a go-go boy."

"Was that it?" I asked, tracing the ripple of his triceps with my fingertips.

"I used to do porn," he said. "I made porn videos."

"Knew that," I said, reaching up to massage the golden arches of Joe's bulging trapezius muscles through his tight white T (tight white Ts were obviously a kind of uniform for him). That morning, following breakfast and prior to leaving for church, I had done a wee bit of Internet research on Joe's film career. Apparently, Joey Lee Turner had never been a top-shelf star in the gay fuck-film firmament, but he had appeared in several successful videos for a few different studios, resulting in an impressive number of Google hits. This mattered to me not a whit.

"And," he said, taking me by the wrists and removing my hands from his shoulders. I took to stroking his smooth caramel forearms. "And, until very recently, I was—" Joe's eyes averted mine. "—I was a call boy," he said, quickly and loudly.

"Stands to reason," I said, strumming my thumb around the general vicinity of Joe's left nipple until I felt it pop up like the built-in timer on a Butterball turkey. I mean, if you're making gay porn, it's better than even money that you're also a masseur-slash-escort-slash—the Greeks had more than one word for it. And frankly, you can't swing a dead cat on Santa Monica Boulevard between Robertson Boulevard and La Brea Avenue on a Saturday night without slapping two or three current or former call boys upside the head.

Joe shot me a lip-pursing look and put his hand over his breast. "And I'm HIV-positive," he said.

I dropped my hands, feeling the wave of emotion—part sympathy, part pity, a dash of relief, and just a *soupçon* of survivor's guilt—that I always felt upon hearing that someone I know is infected with HIV. I waited for it to pass, and then applied a little smile to my face which I hoped sufficiently masked it. I also couldn't help wondering just what all of Joe's ever-watching angels might have been doing while some stud was pumping him full of HIV-infected spooge. Do angels take coffee breaks?

"So how's your health, overall?" I asked.

"Good," he said, his eyes never leaving mine. "Decent T-cells, undetectable viral load."

"Meds?"

"One pill a day. Trizivir. I'm in a trial."

I cupped Joe's beautiful boy face with my hands.

"Thank you for telling me," I said. "But the fact is, I assume every gay man I meet is HIV-positive and conduct myself accordingly. Whatever level of risk I decide is acceptable, I take on that basis." I kissed Joe's mouth, softly, my lips barely brushing his. "Okay?" I said.

Joe nodded. "Okay."

"I trust that's all?"

He nodded again.

I said, "So, could we get back to the kissing part now?"

Fortunately, we were able to pick up pretty much where we'd left off.

"I want to make this good for you," Joe said. I was seated naked at the edge of Joe's single bed. I could feel the chenille bedspread imprinting its knobby pattern into the cheeks of my ass. Joe stood in front of me wearing only white 2Xist briefs (the official underwear of the West Hollywood gay boy, having supplanted Calvin Kleins some time in the late 1990s), his fat hard-on making an intriguing bulge (and a dollar-sized wet spot) in the front of those underpants. He was smiling with lips slightly swollen from several minutes of rather athletic kissing. He was prettier than anything I could imagine. He was stroking my hard dick with both hands.

"Not to worry," I said. "This is good for me."

"No," he said, making a motion like a socket joint with the hollow of one hand and the head of my dick. "I mean, I really want to give you something. Like you gave me last night."

"What did I give you last night?" I asked.

Joe let go of my penis, leaving it feeling cold and not a little bit lonely.

"I've seen you onstage," he said. "I've heard you sing. You can make a whole roomful of people laugh or cry or just feel good, all at once, with your clothes on. You have talent. Maybe I do, too, I don't know yet. The only thing I know for sure that I have is this body."

"Joe," I said, running the fingertips of one hand lightly down his naked torso, just barely touching his clavicle, his perfect pectorals, the finely delineated ripples of his belly. "Lots of people can sing. Relatively few mortals can boast a bod like this one."

Joe smiled, may actually have blushed a bit, and said, "Thanks. That makes me ... thank you." He turned his back to me and lowered his undershorts. He bent from the waist and pulled the briefs down to his knees, revealing (without question) the most beautiful ass I have ever seen.

While I spent my entire ten-year relationship with my late husband, Keith, doing a better-than-average impression of a bottom (deferring to Keith's superior size and nearly insatiable desire to pound my butt until I spoke in unknown languages), the fact is, I'm a top by nature. I harbor a fondness for the male derriere bordering on fixation. And Joe Callahan's ass was prettier than many men's faces. High and round and nearly obscenely protuberant, it was the sort of behind usually found on African-American track runners and dancers (see, Dre), seldom on white men of any ilk: Joe undoubtedly had his black mother to thank for that ass. Given the first opportunity, I had every intention of thanking her myself.

I may have cried out, made some involuntary noise of utter amazement and awe, because Joe turned, looked into my face, and smiled.

I whispered, "Oh my God," and slid from the bed onto my knees: this wasn't just sex—this was worship. I nuzzled Joe's ass, my eyes closed, humming a soft, one-note, wordless song of praise deep down in my throat. I rubbed the cheeks of my face against the cheeks of Joe's butt, kissed each cheek and then gave it a secret name. I licked a long line up each cheek (first left, then right) with the flat of my tongue, then bit the left one just hard enough to leave little scalloped marks on the soft, hairless skin. Joe bent low from the waist, grasping his ankles like a Catholic schoolboy preparing for corporal punishment, exposing the tiny pleats and gathers of his asshole, subtly fragrant and very nearly the exact color and gloss of a chocolate Tootsie Roll Pop. I was excited to the point of trembling. I traced the perimeter of Joe's anus with a fingertip, then tapped on it like a friendly neighbor calling at the back door. I watched Joe's butthole open up and out like some sort of burnt-sugar rose at my touch. My tongue was inside him almost before I realized what I was doing, spreading him apart with my fingers, grunting at the funk and heat and flavor of him. And as my lust-muddled mind struggled to formulate the words to ask, to request, to *beg* for that ass, if it came to that, Joe leaned forward, away from me, leaving my abandoned lips and tongue to kiss and lick at the air. He whispered my name.

I made an odd, animal sound, the power of speech having apparently deserted me for the moment.

And Joe said, "Please fuck me."

Please, he said. Who could refuse such a polite young man?

I wrestled with the Magnum's foil wrapper and then with the condom itself, as if my fingers had suddenly been replaced by ten big toes, until Joe came to my rescue, deftly rolling the latex sheath over my hard-on (a thing so grotesquely engorged I scarcely recognized it) with his blunt but surprisingly nimble fingers. He got up on all fours and said, "Please, Daddy."

I scraped my knees raw on the nubbly bedspread, Joe rocking back into me, shouting (in that balls-deep, husky voice of his) encouragements so nasty I shivered. I tested the muscular, bone and connective-tissue strength of my middle-aged legs, arms, and back doing Joe standing up—Joe up in my arms, his fine, big legs wrapped around my waist, his arms around my neck, bouncing him against my pelvis. I lay back on Joe's bed and took it easy for awhile, watching Joe raise and lower himself on my painfully swollen, latex-encased dick, Joe's head rolling back, his cock hard as the headboard and curved back against his belly, its shiny red-brown noggin painting his abs with little stickywet stripes.

Joe sat down hard and stayed where he sat, his eyes closed and his lips curled into a little smile. He gasped a short breath and then said, "Oh ... fuck," as his dick spurted and then poured like a little fountain, and the sight and sound of it all spurred my own orgasm. I imagine the noise I made (an uncharacteristic beastly growl-and-roar that left both my throat and chest feeling raw) was heard throughout Joe's apartment building, and perhaps throughout West Hollywood in its entirety—rattling the glassware at the French Market Place, rustling the pages of the boycake magazines at A Different Light bookstore, and briefly startling the dudes slurping up one-dollar Margaritas at Mickey's.

After, I lay on my back, my breath still ragged, pulse pounding in my temples, wondering what day it was, wondering if I'd be able to walk without crutches, wondering if perhaps this was how Jacob felt after having spent a long, hot night wrestling with an angel. Joe was lying on top of me, sticky belly to sticky belly, his breath warm against the side of my face.

Joe flicked at my earlobe with his tongue. "So," he said softly, "was I worth the wait?"

Some time later (minutes, days, time had no meaning), I lay wrapped around Joe's impossibly hard-muscled body, legs entangled, both of us damp and smelling of fresh fuck and me feeling about as good as I could remember feeling since the Clinton administration. My dick was nestled in the humid cleft of Joe's ass; amazingly, I hadn't gone soft, as if Joe's succulent youth were somehow contagious. Joe arched his back, pushing his butt back against me, and said, "Damn, you feel good."

"Sure do," I said.

"I can't believe you're so old," he said.

My body stiffened and drew away from him before I'd even realized it. Joe said, "I'm sorry. That's not *exactly* what I meant to say."

"S'okay," I said, moving in closer again. "I'm pretty fuckin' old."

"It's just a number."

"Remember that when you're forty-eight."

"When you're HIV-positive," he said, "you don't automatically assume you're going to get older."

I hugged Joe hard, fiercely, tight as I could. I heard myself grunt with the effort.

"You'll live to be a hundred," I said, almost believing it. After a moment, I said, "You're right, of course. Any gay man who lives to be middle-aged should say thank you, Jesus. I know a lot of people who didn't get this far. Lotta people." I felt a slight twinge of pain in my right testicle. "Still and all," I added as the little *schmertz* dissipated, "I've been young and I've been middle-aged, and believe me, young is better."

Apparently, Joe found no argument for that one. Neither of us said anything for a while. We just lay there, me stroking Joe's smooth skin at various points on his pluperfect anatomy, nuzzling the back of his head and breathing in the warm-cookie sweetness of his hair.

"What cologne are you wearing?" I asked him.

"It's body oil," he said. "I have it custom-mixed for me at Ebba, over on Melrose. It's vanilla and coconut, mostly." Ah—hence the overall sense of fresh-baked goodness, which only added to the already formidable sensation that Joe Callahan (like something out of a fairytale—Hans Christian Andersen by way of Kristen Bjorn) was made entirely of caramel. "Do you like it?" I licked the salty humidity from the nape of Joe's neck and said, "Hell, yeah."

From the computer speakers, I could hear the unmistakable ringing guitar intro from "Maggie May" by Rod Stewart, and then the equally unmistakable Stevie Wonder vocal of "Uptight (Everything's Alright)," sung over the guitar accompaniment of the Rod Stewart number. I didn't even recall Joe having put music on. I pushed myself up on my elbow—just about the only thing that can distract me from really good sex is really good music.

"What is this?" Joe turned to face me.

"It's a mash-up of Rod Stewart and Stevie Wonder."

I felt my lips raising in a smile as Stevie's vocal soared over the unrelated guitar backup, as naturally and seamlessly as if they'd been recorded together. I listened to almost the entire song before speaking again. "Mash-up," I repeated. "Like a remix."

"It is a remix," Joe said, as the song faded out, giving way to "By Your Side" by Sade. "I have lots. I'll burn you a CD."

Then a sudden, solid baby-kick to my right nut, and I winced. Joe reached up and touched my shoulder. "You okay?"

"Fine," I said, deep breathing through the ache in my groin.

"Sure?"

"Sure," I said.

"Good," Joe said, then turned over and presented me his broad back and pornographic former-callboy haunches. "Now get over here and fuck me some more."

An email from Joe was waiting for me when I got home. The subject line read: *I'm tired of buying dinners for younger men*—a Lucille Ball line from *Stage Door*. The body of the email: *You're awesome. I'd really like to see you again. What are you doing this weekend? Terry Randall.* Terry Randall being the name of Kate Hepburn's character. I quickly responded, changing the subject line to read, *Tired little boy with a dream* (an Adolphe Menjou line), and typed in the email body, *How about Saturday night? Dinner and Stage Door? The Great Anthony Powell.* I pressed Send, and the sound of Amos and Andy's stereo meow reminded me I'd neither fed them nor scooped out their box. I hadn't made it all the way up from the chair when a new email popped into my inbox. Subject: *I'm very fond of dinner.*

5.

Monday morning was like the Monday after a ten-day gay cruise to the deep Caribbean: post-vacation letdown. That's how finger-lickin' good it had been with Joe. I'd gone to bed at 8:30 Sunday night (I was tired—and I mean Madeline Kahn "everything below the waist is *kaput*" tired), but I still had to drag my ass out of bed the next morning. I shuffled to the bathroom like Redd Foxx in *Sanford and Son*: my quads and glutes were burning sore and my lower back ached. After putting in my contact lenses, I noticed a lone wild hair had sprouted from the top of my right ear; it was blinding white and about three inches long, waving like the radio aerial on top of a Winnebago.

What is it about midlife and hair? You lose it where you want to keep it, and grow it in places you never imagined—often overnight. Several weeks earlier, I'd spotted these two long, long white hairs growing out of my ballsac. I wrapped them around my finger and gave them a yank, only to discover they were apparently attached to my spinal cord. I experienced a sharp pain, and then lost all feeling in my legs. Like an epidural.

I pulled my tweezers out of the vanity drawer and plucked the ear antenna, hoping to high heaven it hadn't been there the day before for Joe to see.

I was about twenty minutes late getting out of the house and the Monday morning traffic was a horror flick. Ongoing road work on Santa Monica Boulevard had rendered all routes from Mar Vista to Century City nigh unto impossible, turning a five-mile distance into a forty-five-minute ordeal. The eastbound I-10 freeway was a still life and Santa Monica Boulevard no better; but I had a compilation of mash-ups Joe had given me playing on the iPod. I was close enough to work to see the top floors of my building in the distance, as I was riding the brake and doing the pigeon-neck dance to "Kick In the Door" by Biggie mixed with "Runaround Sue" by Dion and The Belmonts, and wondering how people think this shit up, when my cell phone rung "Bewitched." As it was 8:25 on a Monday morning and I wasn't expecting a call, I assumed it was a wrong number as I flipped the phone open.

An unfamiliar male voice said, "Johnnie Ray Rousseau?"

"Yes?"

"My name is Stan. I'm a friend of Lou's. I think we may have met at a party at Lou and Bronco's." And I thought, Shit. No. Not now. "I'm sorry to call so early, but I have a lot of calls to make. I have bad news."

"Louie," I said, "is he gone?"

"Late last night," Stan said. I felt my hands trembling. I gripped the steering wheel hard with my left hand, nearly dropping the phone in my right.

And I said, "Give me just a moment, will you?" I put the phone onto the passenger seat and pulled the Honda over in front of the Nuart Theatre. "Sorry." I could hear someone, another man, talking in the background.

Then Stan said, "Bronco asked me to tell you, Lou wanted you to sing at his memorial service." I leaned forward and pressed my forehead against the top of the steering wheel until it hurt, and then pressed harder. I could tell I was breathing much too quickly, sucking in too much air, and might well pass out if I wasn't careful. "It's this Saturday, at the house," he said. "Are you okay?"

I blew all the air from my lungs through my mouth, then took in a long breath through my nose, then did it again, by which time I had managed to still the tremors and calm myself down to the point where I could say, "I'm fine."

After a moment, Stan said, "I have a lot of calls to make."

"Yes," I managed, "of course. Tell Bronco of course I'll sing. And," I tasted my tears, "and I'm so, so sorry."

I wrestled my handkerchief from my pants pocket and wiped my wet face, then cried until it was soaking wet. When I finally checked the digital dashboard clock, I realized I'd been parked for nearly half an hour with the engine running and the stereo on: Peggy Lee was singing "Fever" over the rhythm track from Elvis Costello's "Watching the Detectives" when I began inching my car back into the creeping traffic to begin the long stop-and-go trip back to my house.

Screw work. I'd call Harold when I got home.

By the time I managed to pull out onto the Boulevard, I'd decided, No: I wasn't going home. I continued eastward. I said "office" into my cell phone and left a voice mail for Harold. I wasn't feeling well and wouldn't be coming in.

I'd known Louie for twenty-six years, since he was eighteen years old, a ruddy-cheeked, round-assed blond boy-thing and I an older man of twenty-two. He was bussing tables at this frowsy little joint in Venice where I was working my first cabaret gig. We hooked up within hours of our first meeting—or so I remembered it later; dated off-and-on; lost touch for a period of years; then reconnected and dated off-and-on some more. We became fuck-buds, roommates, and finally dear friends. But oddly enough, never partners. I'm not sure why. Maybe the timing was never quite right. Louie had been partnered up with Bronco for thirteen years, and for thirteen years I hadn't seen so very much of Louie, largely due to the fact that I didn't much like Bronco. Nor was Bronco particularly crazy about me. It isn't like we fought or anything—we just didn't have chemistry.

But Bronco and I had been forced to endure one another's company on something like a regular basis for the past few years, since Louie took sick. In my observation, we gay men of a certain age who have managed to dodge the HIV bullet tend to go around with the mistaken impression that nothing short of kryptonite can fell us; and can be taken quite by surprise when, say, prostate cancer, decides to pay a visit. In Louie's case, it was a perpetually painful dose of diverticulitis. Unfortunately, Louie chose to self-anesthetize his nearly constant abdominal discomfort with Absolut vodka and, in conjunction with his prescription meds, his liver was reduced to a useless mass in what seemed like record time.

The last time I'd seen Louie, I could hardly find the beautiful boy I'd known in the misshapen old man he had become. He was forty-four years old, and looked a sick seventy-seven. His face had fallen in on itself, sunken skin clinging to cheekbones and collapsed around eye sockets. His teeth looked huge. Louie was folded into one of the two red leather armchairs in the smallish living room of the late-1930s two-story he shared with Bronco in Bixby Knolls, an older, suburb-ish section of Long Beach that had recently become an enclave of domestically inclined pairs of lesbians and gay men. Louie's spindly arms and spidery hands rested atop a belly that looked as if he were hiding a beach ball under his extra large T-shirt.

"Fluid," he began, his voice a rasp so rough it made my own throat ache. Bronco stopped him with a squeeze of his shoulder.

"The fluid the liver would normally filter collects in his abdomen," Bronco explained. Bronco—tall, long-muscled, and handsome in a distinctly Semitic way (the name his *mamaleh* gave him was Stanley Myron Schenkelberg)—had become his partner's nurse, caregiver, and, apparently, mouthpiece. "Can I get you anything, baby?" he asked Louie, ruffling Louie's short, unkempt hair. It was then that I noticed that Louie's hair had either turned grey suddenly or he had been coloring it and I'd never known.

"No," Louie rasped. "Not a baby!" he added, swatting at Bronco's hand as if it were a pesky horsefly. Bronco's face registered pain (as if he'd been punched in the stomach) and heaven only knew what else. He took a half step away from Louie's chair and said to me, "Every few weeks, they perforate his abdomen and drain the fluid. The last time, it nearly killed him." So Bronco had explained when he'd called me a few days before, letting me know that Louie had taken a turn for the worse and that it might be wise to visit sooner rather than later.

"Almost died," Louie whispered, maybe to himself.

"Have you had lots of visitors?" I asked.

Bronco shook his head, mouthed "No," and then said, "I'm going to have a cocktail. How about you?" It was only about two in the afternoon, but I said, "Hell, yes."

He crouched in front of Louie and said, "I'm going to make Johnnie and me a cocktail."

"I'm not deaf," Louie snapped. Bronco let that one pass, and I followed him into their tiny but well-equipped kitchen.

"Attention must not be paid," Bronco said, pulling a large bottle of Absolut from the freezer.

"I know," I said. I had, of course, had a certain amount of firsthand experience with the mood swings of the terminally ill.

He indicated the bottle with a tilt of his head and I nodded my approval. "Nobody wants to visit dying people," he said, opening the refrigerator, "it's a downer." He took a large plastic bottle of Ocean Spray from the fridge. "Cranberry juice okay?" Bronco asked from in front of the open fridge.

"Fine."

Bronco pushed several prescription bottles aside on the tile counter with his big, sinewy hands, making room for the vodka and juice bottles. I noticed at least three miniature bottles marked "Tincture of Morphine." The small dining table outside the kitchen was also covered with similar bottles. If you've laid in a supply of morphine in your kitchen, you're just waiting for the Fat Lady to sing: it's all about making the patients as comfortable as possible while they die.

Bronco took a couple of highball glasses from the cabinet above the counter. "The only real hope he's got is a liver transplant," he said, speaking quickly and quietly, just above a whisper, holding a glass in each hand. "And he's not even on the fucking *list*. So they'll poke another hole in him next week and drain him. There's been some talk about an interim surgery of some kind, but he's not nearly strong enough for that."

I took a step toward Bronco. "Look, Bronc: I know we've never been close. You and I both know that if you weren't married to one of my oldest friends, we most likely wouldn't even know each other." Bronco set the glasses down and faced me. "But I want you to know, I think you're a hero." I lifted a hand to the drug-littered table. "All this," I said, "I don't know if I could do it."

"Thank you," he said, a tear tumbling down his stubbly cheek. He moved toward me and I was in his arms almost before I knew it. "Thank you."

When Bronco and I got back to the living room, cocktails in hand, Louie said, "Sing for me."

Bronco said, "What?" but I knew a command performance when I saw one. Stupidly, I had left the house without a guitar, and I pointed out to Louie that I had no accompaniment.

He said, "Don't care." I sat my drink on the glass-top coffee table and pulled a dining chair up as close to Louie as I could without sitting on his legs. I rested my hands on Louie's bony knees, and Louie tilted his head back and closed his eyes as I sang, "Who knows how long I've loved you?" By the time I finished the song, Louie's face was wet and so was mine.

I had passed Century City and was halfway through Beverly Hills as I recalled the look on Louie's face as I said goodbye to him that afternoon. I'd pressed his hands, kissed his forehead, and promised to be back soon. And he frowned, like a character in a cartoon, his lips making a big upside-down "U." He probably knew we'd never see one another again.

By the time I pulled into the parking lot behind the Flex Complex on Melrose, I'd driven through two separate and distinct crying jags and one red light. I hadn't been to the baths in years, but it had been this one, and it had been fun. It was Monday morning, but there were several cars in the lot: horniness knows no calendar and a hard cock no wristwatch.

I paid for a locker (I had no need for a room—I wasn't planning to set up housekeeping) and as I pushed my clothes into it, I silently regretted my having no sandals with me, but I figured barefoot would probably get me more ass than naked-with-penny-loafers.

Standing in front of the first room on the left upon entering the main hallway was an impressively muscled thirty-something with a sandy-blond flat-top haircut and reddish beard stubble outlining a strong jaw and cleft chin. A chunky but not unattractive Latino was chatting him up. I slowed my pace slightly as Flat-Top and I exchanged glances. He turned away from Latino Guy and said, "Sup?"

"Sup?" I repeated, first to Flat-Top, then his companion.

Flat-Top inclined his close-cropped head to the slightly opened doorway of the room and said, "Wanna come in?" I glanced at Latino Guy (who looked a tad miffed), shrugged, and said, "Sure." I started to follow Flat-Top into the room and, apparently, the other man made a move to follow me because Flat-Top lifted his hand in a traffic-cop *Stop* sign (or maybe it was a Diana Ross *Stop* sign) and said, "Just him."

I closed the door to the claustrophobic cubicle behind me, removed my towel, and hung it on the doorknob. Flat-Top said, "Damn," and reached down to stroke my dick (which had gone hard before he'd finished saying "Wanna"). Within seconds, the guy was in full squat in front of me, taking my dick down his throat. He was no beginner. Once my eyes adjusted to the dim light, I noticed a big pump-bottle of Gun Oil lube and several wrapped condoms on the built-in excuse for a bed-table next to the built-in excuse for a bed. I reached over and snagged a condom and tapped the guy lightly on the top of his head with it.

"Help me on with this, willya?"

He smiled and said, "Fuckin'-A."

I fucked him hard, his big weightlifter legs up over my shoulders, yanking his chubby dick until he spurted into his chest-and belly-hair. We actually cuddled a bit afterward, spooned into the hard, narrow cot, my half-hard nestled into the humid fuzz in the guy's asscrack.

"Do you always say that right after you come?" he said after a few minutes.

"Do I always say *what?*"

"'I'm alive.'"

I swear I didn't remember any such thing. "Not as a rule, no."

Clara always taught me not to overstay, so after a couple more minutes, I kissed the guy on top of his head and we hugged a good warm one and I said, "Thank you."

When I emerged from the room, Latino Guy was still outside, back against the wall, well-built legs crossed at the ankles, making a nice little calf-muscle show.

He looked at me and said, "You fucked him, didn't you?"

I said, "Yeah."

A raise of one eyebrow and one corner of his full lips. "Isn't he the lucky one."

I shrugged and said, "Got a room?"

I made sure to thank him afterward. The next guy, too.

I spent the remainder of the day on my sofa, watching epic movies on DVD: *Gone with the Wind*, followed by *Titanic*, and finally, *Maurice*. I wasn't the least bit hungry (I've never been a stress eater)—though I might have gnawed on a PowerBar at some point; but my depression was not so debilitating that I didn't manage to feed my cats and scoop out the box. For their part, Amos and Andy seemed to take one-and-a-half to two-hour turns curling up against me on the sofa, like nurses alternating shifts.

During *Maurice*, as Alec Scudder climbed in through the window and surprised Maurice in bed, I thought about how my old UCLA Men's Glee Club buddy Kenny Watson had slept with his second-floor bedroom window open, summer and winter, for years, in case his own Alec Scudder might choose to climb in some night. The one time a man did enter through Kenny's window, it wasn't for romance: he stole Kenny's CD boombox and wallet. Kenny died of AIDS complications in the summer of 1998, after conventional wisdom held that nobody was dying of AIDS anymore. But Kenny had been diagnosed in 1985 and in the course of thirteen years, he'd dined on every medicinal combo-plate on the menu and nothing worked anymore.

I cried through all of Ben Kingsley's scenes in *Maurice*—not my favorite part of the movie, anyway—and by the time Alec was making noises like he was going to blackmail Maurice, I'd had enough, and dragged my ass off the couch and into bed. It was nearly midnight and I'd had a bad day.

Tuesday morning, I woke up around eight, not having set my alarm. I rolled over in bed, and called the office, confident that I would get Harold's voice mail. My first-thing-in-the-morning voice has always made for a good imitation of a not-feeling-so-hot voice, so I was pretty sure my voice message that I still wasn't feeling up to going into work would sound convincing. I made a point of not claiming to be sick, which would have been a lie—only that I didn't feel up to working, which was true.

I spent Tuesday in its entirety in my not-quite-clean terrycloth robe and suede slippers, never even bothering to shower. By the time I was relatively conscious, I realized my unexpected fast the day before had rendered me ravenous. After filling Amos and Andy's food bowls, I cooked up a six-egg-white omelet and some oatmeal and ate in bed, watching TV.

For some reason (or maybe no reason at all), it was Judy Garland day on Turner Classic Movies. I killed the better part of the day watching some of Judy's lesser-known work—*Listen, Darling* with Mary Astor and Robert Sinclair (who was British and kind of cute in that pale, rather anemic-looking way British boys can be cute), followed by *Presenting Lily Mars* with Van Heflin (whom I'd always considered just a shout away from butt-ugly, but who suddenly seemed rather appealing this time around), followed by *Strike Up the Band* with Mickey Rooney (who, of course, was the number-one box office draw for like the entirety of the 1930s, which I've never understood, but I guess you had to be there). Before and after each film, with commentary and trivia, was dear old Robert Osborne, portly and cheerful, his round, avuncular face emerging from what looked to be a too tight shirt-collar. Robert always seemed like such a sweet old Auntie as he divulged such delicious dream factory trivia as the fact that Mary Astor, Judy's mother in *Listen, Darling*, also played Judy's mother in *Meet Me in St. Louis*. Just the sort of bullshit I pretty much live for. I pictured myself in ten years, a trivia-spewing Auntie, a chocolate Robert Osborne without a TV show.

The phone rang in the middle of the "How About You" number in *Strike Up the Band*. I considered letting it roll over to the machine, but finally muted the TV and grabbed the phone on the fourth ring. I made sure my hello was appropriately raspy, in case it was Harold needing to find a file or something.

"I called your office," Clara said, without preamble. "They said you were sick."

"Ma," I said. "How are you? Good to hear from you. How are you?"

"Not bad," she said. "Right now. Check with me in an hour. You sick or playing hooky?"

I leaned back into the pillows. Judy mimed the ballad while Mickey played silent piano, but I'd seen it so many times I could hear the music in my head. I weighed the option of telling Clara about my two friends' premature deaths within a week of one another. Whining to a lady with a brain tumor, who was probably spending her more enjoyable hours throwing up, seemed childish—despite my actually being her child. Finally, I said, "I lost a couple of friends this week. One AIDS, one liver failure. Frankly, I'm a little depressed. So I gave myself the day off, been watching TV all morning." I glanced at the bedside clock: it was one-thirty—I'd been watching TV longer than "all morning."

"Judy Garland on Turner Classic?" she said.

I had to laugh. "Guilty." I closed my eyes and pictured my mother's deeply dimpled face. "So, how are you really?"

"Weak," she said after a moment. "Aching. Hard to keep anything down. This radiation is kicking my behind. Good news is, my behind hasn't been this small since I was in high school." That's my mama: vain to the bone.

"I've put you on the prayer list at my church," I said.

She said, "Prayer changes things," and I knew she really believed that. "I'll be praying for you, too. It's hard, losing people." I decided to withhold comment on the obvious irony. "You singing at the funerals?" she asked.

"God, yes."

"That's hard," she said. And at once, we both said, "Can't grieve."

We shared a small, sad laugh.

"Well," she said after we finished chuckling, "watch out for the third one."

"The third what?"

"Well, you know," she said, "these things come in threes."

"And don't walk under ladders," I said.

"Laugh if you want," she said, "but I'm telling you."

"All right, then," I said. "Threes." Then I changed the subject. "I want to see you. When can I come see you?"

"I'm sorry," she said, "about before. I was just feeling so bad, puking all the time. I just didn't want to see anybody, didn't want anybody to see me. Not even Daniel, but I didn't have much choice." She cleared her throat a couple of times, and then said, "I think this weekend should be okay."

"I've got Louie's funeral on Saturday," said. "Could I come down Saturday evening, afterward?"

"What about church?"

"I'm not on the altar this Sunday," I said, which wasn't true, but I'd call Pastor Tom and beg off.

"Think you'll be here for dinner?" she asked.

I said, "No, I don't think so." I could just see her if I'd said yes, up in the kitchen, rattling them pots and pans. I heard a click on the line.

"That's my call waiting," Clara said.

"I'll let you go then," I said quickly. As I've likely mentioned, I detest call waiting. "I'll see you Saturday. I love you."

"Love you," she said, and click—she was gone.

And then I remembered: I'd have to break my Saturday date with Joe Callahan. I was rolling myself out of bed to get to the computer and find Joe's phone number when the phone, still in my hand, rang again.

"Hey, Shorty." Dre. "I called your office, they said you was out sick. You okay?" I explained, somewhat hurriedly, about Louie's death and the prospect of singing at another funeral (though I admit to leaving out the story of my field trip to the baths). "Damn," he said. "That's some shit."

"And the church said, Amen."

"You want some company?" he asked.

"I don't think so, babe." I would have had to shower, floss, and brush my teeth just to approximate humanity, and I was in no mood to bother. Besides, I still felt pretty much like hell, and Turner Classic held the promise of *Summer Stock*, with the "Get Happy" number and Gene Kelly's monumental dancer's ass in snug-fitting chinos. Not nearly as good as Dre's monumental dancer's ass live and in person, but Gene wouldn't care if I still had first-thing-in-the-morning bad breath in the late afternoon. "I appreciate the offer, though."

"Call me if you change your mind," he said.

I had scarcely hung up before I considered calling Dre right back and taking him up on his offer. I picked up the receiver, but then changed my mind again. I'd call Dre soon and set up something, maybe for the weekend.

I got up, retrieved Joe's phone number, called, and got voice mail. I left a typical Rousseauian too-long, too-fast, too-much-information message (I never know how much time I've got and it never fails to make me nervous), and then climbed back into bed and Judy'd myself into a near-stupor well into the evening.

I managed to drag my ass into the office the next morning. There was little more than some filing awaiting me on my two-days-neglect-ed desk, and I arrived to a voice mail message from Harold claim-ing that he was feeling a bit under the weather and would be staying home; and an email from Joe (subject: *the trap-door, the humidor and the cuspidor*) requesting a reschedule of our movie date. So all things considered, Wednesday didn't shape up into a particularly high-stress day; and except for having to choose songs for Louie's memorial service (two Beatles numbers—"In My Life" and "I'll Follow the Sun"), and unpack my pathetically underutilized Yamaha six-string to practise them in the evenings, the rest of the week turned out to be a smear of normality: office, gym, and home; office, gym, and home. But it was just a false alarm, or a false lack of alarm.

As it turned out, Mama didn't lie. These things do come in threes.

It was Friday, late morning, about an hour before lunch time, when Number Three rolled into town. Vince, the file clerk with whom I shared a double secretarial bay, was explaining *bukkake*, which is apparently a Japanese term for when a group of men gather around and shoot their man-goo into the face of one supine woman. I have no idea how the subject came up. True, it comes as no surprise to *moi* that such goings-on go on, but it somehow seemed peculiarly Japanese to have a special name for it.

"I can't really get off watching that shit," Vince said. He was two-hole punching documents with determined, guillotine-like strokes and skewering them into a powder-blue pressboard folder. He was twenty-nine years old (see, Young Enough to Be My Child), cute as a Hostess cupcake, and tragically heterosexual. His short, meticulously spiked dark hair and topiary goatee bespoke a young man who'd qualify as metrosexual if only he had the budget. As things were, Vince's gym-pumped biceps bulged from the short sleeves of a black T-shirt imprinted with electric-green "code" from *The Matrix*. He was saying, "I *totally* don't get off on that, dude," as I checked my personal email for maybe the thirty-seventh time that day, just in case Joe Callahan might have dropped a line since the thirty-sixth time I'd checked. I Cheshire-cat grinned at the sight of an email in my box with the subject: *The chair Bernhardt sat in*—yeah, another reference from that movie of ours.

Vince continued, "Because usually, you can just tell the woman doesn't really *want* to have half a dozen guys knocking off knuckle babies in her face." By this time, he'd stopped hole-punching for a bit, pausing to reach underneath his T-shirt to scratch his chest, exposing a broad stripe of pale-skinned, dark-fuzzed belly—why must straight boys do that?

I double-clicked Joe's email. It read: *Hate my job. Rehearsals frustrating. Wish I was seeing you this weekend. Getting a chub just thinking about you. J.*

Thinking about Joe getting a chub was enough to launch a bone of my own. Vince said, "And her face is all pinched up, like she's about to get slapped or something, and you just know she's only about nineteen, twenty years old, and she's probably thinking, 'Fuck, I wanted to be an *actress*! I played Juliet in high school, for crissake!' Ruins the whole thing for me. So I usually change DVDs at that point." Vince's triceps bunched as he shoved the hole-punch down. The mental image of Vince sprawled in front of his TV set, playing with this joystick, wasn't exactly dissipating the swelling in my casual-Friday black jeans.

A new email from Pastor Tom appeared in my inbox, subject: *Sad news.*

"Fuck," I whispered.

"What's up?" Vince asked.

"Don't know yet," I said, opening Tom's email. The message had been addressed to the deacons, with a CC to all the members and friends of Temple of Love Church who had email addresses and didn't mind sharing them with Pastor Tom (and the rest of the congregation, for that matter, since Tom seemed incapable of using BCC): *I am sad to report that our sister, Denise Micheaux, lost her long battle with cancer this morning. Her wife of 30 years, Sharon Lee Bond, was with her. I will keep you apprised of the schedule for the memorial service. Please keep Sharon Lee in your prayers.*

I wasn't particularly close with Sharon Lee and Denise. They were just the salt-and-pepper-haired, middle-aged lesbian couple in the back row of the church, given to stereotypical lesbian outfits of plaid flannel shirts, Dickies workpants, and Birkenstock sandals with socks. True, they had their enemies in the congregation: they sometimes seemed to make a sort of parlor game out of being vocally contrary at the quarterly congregational meetings, and they'd once withheld their tithes for half a year over some disagreement about one of Pastor Tom's sermons.

The overwhelming redeeming quality of this particular couple was that they loved my singing. Anytime I was scheduled to solo, Sharon Lee and Denise would make a point of being there, and they'd usually tap into their own little lesbian grapevine and make sure four or five of their Birkenstocked buddies were in attendance as well. I'd been told (strictly off the record) by the church treasurer that Sharon Lee and Denise upped their collection-plate offering by as much as 100 percent on Sundays when I soloed. And after service, they'd walk up and kiss me, first Denise and then Sharon Lee, engulfing me in their rather dense cologne (whatever it was, they both wore it), their soft post-menopausal mustaches tickling my cheek. Tears stung my eyes as I realized how much I would miss that.

Oh, well, I thought. At least there had been no mention of my singing at the memorial. Even as my diva pride was just the tiniest bit hurt that I had not been asked to sing, at least I'd be able to grieve like a normal person for once. Just then, a new email popped in from Pastor Tom. Subject: *One more thing.* It read, *On her deathbed, Denise requested that you sing Amazing Grace at her funeral.*

Thank God for the gym. Fridays are legs-back-biceps-abs, and that particular Friday I welcomed more than usual the sweet burn of four sets of deep, ass-to-heels squats with a barbell stacked with my approximate bodyweight searing across my shoulders. Following the final set, my glutes and quads spasming, chest heaving with the effort, I leaned on the racked weight bar for support, and I could have sworn I could actually feel my own blood pump.

In my periphery, I caught sight of somebody sidling up to me. I turned to see a sinewy, shaved-head white boy in baggy grey sweats and the ragged remains of a T-shirt. He rested a pale hand on the weight bar, his arm rippling with muscle decorated with spiky, pseudo-tribal tattoos. His smile knew nothing of orthodontia and his English was Aussie accented: "Lookin' good there, Mate," he said through that flawed, sexy grin.

"Thanks," I said, short of breath. "You too." We extended workout-gloved right hands simultaneously and exchanged first names (his was Max). Max then executed a quick squat, unencumbered by barbell, and pulled a card out of his shoe. I took the slightly damp, foot-funky thing between two fingers and tucked it under the waistband of my jock. Max said, "Give me a call sometime, Johnnie," and loped away toward the dumbbell racks, his boyish ass rolling like two grapefruits in a lunch bag.

I smiled and whispered to the weight bar, "I'm alive."

I knew hardly a soul at Louie's memorial service—just Bronco, really. A quick, nearly subconscious head-count (it's an old club-singer habit, I can't help it) indicated maybe twenty-five people, mostly gay men of a certain age, hands full of wine glasses and crustless finger sandwiches, as I shouldered open the front door of Bronco and Louie's home. Correction: Bronco's home. A tall, good-looking brunet with that too-lean poz look, voluntarily relieved me of my guitar as I entered. I'd brought my big Yamaha acoustic and my portable PA system; carrying them the short distance from my car to the front door had caused a painful muscle twinge between my shoulder blades. I set the PA down briefly, shrugged my pained shoulders, then lifted it up again with my left hand as the brunet extended his right and said, "Remember me? Stan. I called you the other day. We've met before."

I smiled, took Stan's hard, sinewy hand and said, "Of course I remember you," though I was none too sure I actually did.

"Why don't you set up over here," he said, indicating a corner of the living room where someone had placed a large easel with a poster board covered with photographs of Louie: elementary school portraits, professional headshots, candids. I spotted a snapshot of Louie and me, shiny and grinning at the cast party of a production of *Godspell* we'd done together in Hollywood in 1980-something (I'd sung "All Good Gifts"; Louie had portrayed the Savior Himself, pretty beyond all fairness, with a greasepaint valentine heart painted on his forehead). Jesus H., we were so young.

As I was unlatching the PA speakers, Bronco approached with a small entourage I could recognize at a glance as Louie's immediate family: a smallish couple in their seventies—the man a senior version of Louie (though younger looking than Louie had been the last time I'd seen him); the woman might have been played by Shirley Jones in the movie of Louie's life: matronly but fit-looking, wearing the face she had been painting on since her twenties, her pixie-cut hair professionally colored to approximate the hair color of her youth. Bronco was in busy widower mode, his face unreadable as he introduced us. Louie's mother might have been Susan, maybe not, and I couldn't tell you his dad's name at the point of a gun. I clasped their hands and stammered something I hoped was at least polite. When the mother said, "Louis mentioned how much he loved your singing," all I could manage was, "Yes," and then, "I really need to set up."

It wasn't much of a service, as services go. Thankfully, there was no *corpus*: Louie had been cremated the day after his death. Bronco said a few words; Louie's dad tried to speak, but mostly wept into a crumpled, damp excuse for a handkerchief. I don't think any of the friends (an ill-at-ease platoon in a uniform of dark slacks and open-collared dress shirts) said anything, though Bronco repeatedly asked them to. I sang and finger-picked my way through one song at the beginning and one at the end, with scattered sniffles from those assembled accompanying the final chord of "I'll Follow the Sun." And that was that.

As I slipped the Yamaha back into the case, I sensed someone standing behind me. I stood and looked up to face a very tall, rawboned, probably thirty-something man wearing khaki pants, a white button-down shirt with the collar flopping loose, and a reasonable facsimile of Louie's face. I had somehow missed him completely.

He said, "Excuse me," through barely parted lips. "I'm Mark. Louis's brother." I may have actually frowned with the effort of trying to remember if Louie had ever mentioned he even had a brother. I offered my right hand, but the brother's big mitts hung limp at his sides. "Your singing," he said, and stared down at his probably-size-fifteen Hush Puppies and said, "thank you."

I said, "You're welcome ... Mark." I struggled for a follow-up remark and finally said, "I loved your brother."

"So did I," he said in a raspy whisper. "But I never told him."

I only realized I had been addressing Mark's footwear when I watched a wet spot appear on the beige suede toe of his right shoe. I looked up at a face all but folded in half with quiet weeping. In almost any other situation, I would have taken this man into my arms (as well as I could take a six-foot-four dude into my arms), but his posture was forbidding of physical contact even before he covered his eyes with one lengthy, white-shirted arm. I just stood and watched him cry for maybe a minute, a largely silent activity involving his wide, sharp-angled shoulders.

At that moment, I could think of nothing sadder than this: to lose your big brother and realize too late that you'd never said I love you.

I reached up and squeezed his shoulder (a handful of fabric and bone) and said, "I'm sure he knew." Mark nodded vigorously, obviously wanting to believe that at least as much as I did.

I packed my equipment quickly, having no desire to tarry, hastily shoving the PA's power cord and speaker cables into the little trap door in the back of the console, acknowledging the three or four people who made a point of coming up to tell me how much they enjoyed my singing, as succinctly but politely as possible—it always seems essentially wrong to take bows at a funeral. Three-quarters of the way to the front door (so close, so close), Bronco stopped me and offered to roadie my PA out to the car.

I quickly declined. "You have guests," I said.

"This won't take long," he said, wrestling the handle from my grasp. Setting the case down on the curb beside my Honda, Bronco said, "Thank you for doing this. I really appreciate it." He pulled me into his arms and hugged me tight.

I said, "Take care of yourself, Bronco."

"We'll stay in touch," Bronco said, but we both knew better.

Merging onto the eastbound 91, I flipped my cell phone open and said, "Mom." To my surprise, she answered on the second ring.

"Just wanted you to know I'm on my way."

"Okay, baby," she said, sounding very much like her old self. "Be careful on the freeways."

"I will," I said. Then quickly added, "I love you, Ma."

"I love you, too, baby."

Clara answered the door herself, wearing another Afro-print dress, her head wrapped in a matching scarf. Her face looked sunken; or maybe I was imagining it. I hugged her as hard as I could without fear of breaking my mother like an overcooked chicken wing. We walked through the foyer toward the family room, arm in arm.

"How are you, Ma?" I asked. "Really."

She shrugged. "Been better," she said, "and I been worse. Recently. This chemo is cuttin' me a flip."

"Hello, John." As usual, I heard Daniel's voice before I realized he'd entered the room, once again in T-shirt and jeans and no shoes. I couldn't help noticing his big beautiful feet: high arches, long toes. Yeah, I like feet—sue me.

"Hello, Daniel," I extended my right hand and prayed he'd accept it, rather than bear-hugging me. He shook my hand and slapped my shoulder with his left. "I've got some paperwork to deal with," he said, backing away toward the bedrooms. "I'll leave you two alone."

Clara said, "I thank God for that man, every day." She walked me to the sofa. "You hungry?"

"No, thanks," I said, "I picked up a burger on the way here." Which was a lie. I'd high-tailed it over, no stops, and I hadn't had a burger since the mid-80s. I just didn't want to run the risk of Clara doing anything resembling work on my account.

"Want to watch a movie?"

"Sure," I said, falling back into the couch. "What'cha got?"

She indicated a short stack of DVD cases on the glass-topped coffee table. "Daniel rented some this afternoon."

After weighing the pros and cons of the half-dozen new releases Daniel had picked up at the local Blockbuster, we ended up pulling *Ray* out of Clara's collection. I owned it too and had already seen it four or five times, and I'm sure Clara at least matched that, but come on—it's Ray Charles. We munched from a bag of cashew halves, talked back to Jamie Foxx, and supplied extra backup vocals when we felt they were called for (the rag-tag Raelettes on the white leather sofa). About halfway in (Ray was leaving Atlantic Records for ABC), Clara hit the pause button for a potty break. In her absence, I suddenly remembered I'd meant to ask her about something. When she'd settled back into the sofa, I said, "A weird thing happened at church the other day." I told her about suddenly getting sick after praying a blessing over the schizophrenic boy-lover guy. When I was through, my mother shut her eyes and took in a long breath. She placed a warm, paper-dry hand on mine and said, "Lord have mercy! You have it, too."

"Got what?" I said.

She opened her almond eyes, looked deeply into mine, like Maria Ouspenskaya in *The Wolfman*, about to tell Lon Chaney Jr. that he's a "*verevolf*."

"You have the gift of healing," she said, nodding her kerchief'd head slowly up and down. "I have it, so did Mother. I should have guessed you would, too."

And then came the dawn. "Oh, shit" I said. I realized that I should have guessed it first—it made all the sense in the world: back in the 80s, when friends (Crockett Miller included) started falling ill and there was little or no real medical help to be found, I'd been trained in Eastern healing arts and proved to have something of an aptitude for balancing chakras. Of course, I'll never know if I was dealing in large helpings of the placebo effect; but my attitude has always been, whatever makes you feel better. Anyway, I'd fallen out of the whole practice a decade before, once protease inhibitor drugs rode in like the cavalry and began saving hundreds of HIV-positive lives, and then forgot all about it. But tapping into The Source is tapping into The Source, in church or otherwise. And I had apparently tapped.

"Same thing used to happen to me," Clara continued. "I'd pray for somebody's migraines and doggone if I didn't end up with a headache. Pray for somebody with abdominal pain, I'd get a stomachache."

"So," I wondered, "what do you do about it?"

She said, "Wash your hands."

"Wash your hands?" That's it?

"As soon as you can after you pray, wash your hands, thoroughly, with hot water and soap." She shrugged her little shoulders. "Simple as that." She picked up the TV remote and aimed it at the set, but I touched the back of her hand to stop her: I'd had an idea.

I said, "What about you?"

"What?"

I held my hands out, palms up, and said, "Healing."

She looked at me as if she'd never laid eyes on me before, staring into my face for a long moment; then she turned her face away and mumbled something to herself I couldn't hear well enough to understand. And then, without another word, she knelt in front of the sofa like a child saying her good-night prayers, folded her hands, and bowed her head low, eyes closed.

And suddenly I thought, what the hell did I just offer? Who was I all of a sudden? *The Song of* freakin' *Bernadette?* Jennifer Jones with the healing spring and an off-screen choir? A tremble shot through me and my skin became gooseflesh. I took a deep, cleansing breath and blew it out slowly, rubbing the palms of my hands together. Something way deep inside me said, Please, as I encircled my mother's head with my hands.

I have no idea what I might have said, or how long I prayed. I finished when I was finished. I opened my eyes to the sight of my mother's face, her eyes glistening, the corners of her lips just slightly raised.

I all but leapt to my feet and ran to the bathroom to wash my hands.

Part II
Hurricane

6.

Summer seemed like the magic antidote to the shit storm that had been my spring. Weeks, then months went by with no funerals to sing at. To the shock and surprise of Clara's doctors, Clara's husband, Clara's firstborn son—and seemingly everyone but Clara—my mother's inoperable brain tumor had shrunk. In late May, Clara's world-noted oncologist, Dr Roseman, announced to her and Daniel that Clara's tumor had apparently stopped growing. In July, he cautiously opined that it might, in fact, be smaller. By early August, there was no doubt: the tumor had shrunk and was continuing to shrink. Dr Roseman cited the combined effects of radiation, chemo, and cutting-edge drug therapy while Clara herself (who was by this point frighteningly thin and quite bald) simply said, "Prayer changes things." As far as my mother was concerned, God had used her own son's hands to work a genuine water-to-wine, take-up-your-bed-and-walk miracle. For me, I cared not a bit how or why or whether my little barbell-calloused hands were in any way partially responsible, but I thanked my God morning and night that my mother was better. By mutual agreement, Clara, Daniel, and Dr Roseman chose to suspend all of Clara's treatments (save for the growth inhibitor drugs) for the time being—no chemo, no radiation—while regularly monitoring the progress of the tumor.

And as if that wasn't enough, the summer when Clara got better was also the summer when Joe Callahan loved me.

He actually said the three little words for the first time in June. Joe and I had been seeing one another off and on for maybe six weeks, when his schedule of rehearsals, head-shot photo sessions and auditions allowed. Usually, we'd just get together at my place or his for a simple dinner and a DVD, followed by one or more humid fuckings: in bed, on living room sofas, straddling one of my kitchen chairs, slip-and-sliding in Joe's Depression-era bathtub. It didn't take long for me to realize I was falling in love, and even less time to cop to the basic insanity of falling for a guy young enough to be my son. But even having so copped, I made no effort to break my fall.

Joe had been in rehearsal for several weeks for something called *The Naked Truth*. The omni-sexual sex farce in which Joe had been cast back in May had died aborning (as so many little theater productions do), but he had scarcely had time to register the disappointment before he was cast in *The Naked Truth*, a homoerotic meringue of a comedy, full of wisecracks and asscracks: as I discovered from my rather creaky front-row seat on opening night, the entire all-male cast of six ended up mother-naked onstage by the final curtain. To my surprise, my Joe was the apparent star and drawing card for this little enterprise: the posters in front of the theater featured the magnificently naked Joe (billed as "Joe 'Joey Lee Turner' Callahan"), with the play's title emblazoned across his crotch. To my further (and entirely pleasant) surprise, in addition to his oh-so-obvious physical attributes, Joe Callahan also displayed an amusing way with a comic line and a raised eyebrow (imagine, if you can, a naked caramel-colored bodybuilder, channeling Roz Russell). The capacity opening-night audience of ninety-nine applauded loudly and long (to quote George Sanders).

Following a brief reception during which most of the obscenely beautiful cast got sauced on boxed Chablis, Joe and I adjourned to my house and into my bed where we made love between Joe's repeated choruses of "Was I really okay?" and my repeated assurances that he was, in fact, considerably better than okay. Afterward, we lay wrapped around each other, sleep descending on me like a coverlet from heaven, when suddenly Joe said, "Didn't hear from you much this week."

"I know," I said. "I'm sorry. It was," I looked for a definition that didn't seem silly, even though I knew what I'd done had, in fact, been very silly. "It was an exercise."

I had made a point of neither calling nor emailing Joe for three consecutive days before his Friday opening night—not a small project, as Joe and I had fallen into the habit of emailing one another repeatedly throughout the day, just about every day; and besides, I thought about Joe on a nearly constant basis. I chose to cease communication for a while purely as an exercise, to see if I could, if only to prove to myself that I had not morphed into a twelve-year-old schoolgirl, drawing loopy valentine hearts in sparkly red ink around her boyfriend's initials.

Joe pushed away from my embrace and turned in bed to face me. "Don't exercise like that," he said. "Exercise this," he punched me softly in the chest. He grabbed a handful of my ass and said, "Exercise that. I check my fucking email like every half hour, hoping I'll hear from you. I think about you all the damn time. I miss you every day I don't see you."

"I know," I said. "I mean, me too."

"Well, don't do that shit anymore," he said. And I was about to say something, I don't know what, but then I could have sworn Joe said, "I love you."

"What?"

He averted his eyes and said, "Nothing. Never mind. I love you."

"Oh my God." I kissed Joe's fat lips, his nose, eyelids, and lips again, and I said, "Oh my God" again, this time pretty much into Joe's mouth, and then I said it, too: "I love you." And then we made love some more, and said it over and over.

From there, we began using "I love you" like Hawaiians use "Aloha": for hello, goodbye, pass the ketchup; in person, on cell phones, and at the ends of emails, but alas, we used it more in the latter two than the former: *The Naked Truth* took up Joe's evenings from Thursday through Sunday, so scheduling time together proved a challenge. But inconvenience was easily overshadowed by the beauty, the splendor, the wonder of being loved by Joe Callahan. This inappropriately young, unfairly beautiful man loved me. He said so, often and right out loud. And that made just about anything okay.

For awhile, anyway.

I even managed to get Joe to church. He'd been raised Catholic—had been an altar-boy, finger-banged by the parish priest at ten years old, the whole *schmeer*—and had an understandable grudge against church, all church, any church. But the power of love and of a forty-eight-year-old man whining incessantly for weeks proved strong, and

Joe finally agreed to accompany me to Sunday service at Assembly of Love in mid-June.

Dre was ushering that morning and seemed to be in a particularly foul mood; tossing bulletins at Joe and me, Dre grunted in response as I introduced him to Joe.

"Is this the Christian hospitality you've been talking about?" Joe whispered as we walked away.

The rest of my brothers and sisters in faith welcomed Joe with their usual open arms, and while at least some of them must have recognized Joe from his video and print work, no one seemed to treat him differently than any other flawlessly beautiful young man—meaning, there was a certain amount of gushing, and I was free to enjoy the admiration and envy that came with having Joe Callahan on my arm.

Joe and I took communion together: his eyes brimmed with tears as I placed the wafer on his tongue. I knew he'd be back.

Immediately after the service, while Joe was in the restroom, I approached Dre as he gathered up the used programs left on chair seats and dropped to the floor.

"Hey, Dre." He didn't even turn around; he bent down to pick up a hymnal from the floor.

"Wassup, Johnnie?" He almost always calls me Shorty.

"That's kind of what I'm wondering," I said. "Are we okay?"

"Sure," he said, still not facing me. "Why not?"

"Well, you seemed a bit brusque this morning when we came in," I said. "And in case you haven't noticed, you're not looking at me."

Dre finally turned to face me. "Johnnie, I'm busy. As, apparently, are you. Busy, busy, busy." He crumpled the programs in his hand and pointed over my shoulder with them. "Look, here comes your business now."

I turned to see Joe walking toward me. When I turned back, Dre was walking away, across the sanctuary. I called out, but he chose to ignore me, walking a little faster.

"What's with him?" Joe asked.

"I don't know." But of course I knew. It had been weeks since I'd exchanged more than a few words with Dre on the phone, since I'd taken up with Joe. I wasn't seeing much of anyone except Joe—not even the Sullivans. It was just part of courtship. Wasn't it? Dre would understand that. We were friends, after all.

Walking out of the sanctuary hand-in-hand with Joe, I made a quick mental note to give Dre a call. And I really meant to.

Then in late June, Joe talked me into going to Pride. It didn't take much talking—I didn't say no to Joe all that often. I hadn't attended a gay pride fest in years. I'm not good with crowds (at least any crowd not gathered to applaud me), and, not being particularly tall, I recalled Pride as hours of staring at Adam's apples and napes of necks. Besides which, the multitudes of West Hollywood-style masculine physical perfection on display mostly succeeded in making me feel small and plain, and very, very old; a near-formless blob of flesh set atop a pair of high-top sneakers. All that notwithstanding, I would have attended Beelzebub's birthday party in the bowels of hell if Joe had asked me to, so off to West Hollywood I went.

Joe was scheduled to ride on a huge white wedding cake of a float for a local queer bar, smiling and waving and shaking his considerable groove thing nonstop for the duration of the parade: a maddeningly democratic event in which (it seemed) just about anyone who really wanted to, marched. Or rode a convertible. Or a motorcycle. Or a skateboard. Or whatever—the point being that the person or persons at the helm of the parade apparently (like Ado Annie) could not say no to anyone in possession of the entry fee. Which means that the West Hollywood Gay Pride parade historically begins at 11:30 Sunday morning, and ends maybe a week after Yom Kippur. It was my plan to wait for Joe at the parade's end, spend as little time at the Pride festival as possible, and get Joe back to my house and out of the infinitesimal white cotton-spandex shorts he was wearing, as quickly as I could work it.

We parked my Accord in the seemingly endless parking structure of the colossal stack of sapphire Legos that is the Pacific Design Center and began the few blocks walk to the parade starting point. It took mere minutes for me to learn that walking along Santa Monica Boulevard on Pride Day with Joe Callahan was not unlike strolling along the Champs-Elysées wheeling the *Mona Lisa* along behind you on a red Radial Flyer wagon. Roughly every two-point-five steps, some passerby would call out, "Hey Joey," or "Hi Joe," or simply "Dayum!" or "Yum," or express his desire to perform some triple X-rated act (or series of acts) with or upon my Joe that I could only suppose was not only illegal east of the Rockies but also very possibly beyond the actual capability of the human skeletal structure. Between Robertson and San Vicente Boulevards, we were stopped four times by people asking to have their pictures taken next to Joe. Joe Callahan was a parade unto himself. I suppose I should have expected it, but I hadn't. To me, Joe was just my boyfriend—my young, unjustly beautiful boyfriend, to be sure, but I had apparently underestimated his audience. I hadn't felt quite so invisible since before I grew pecs.

"You didn't warn me you were a tourist attraction," I said as we walked away from the fifth cell-phone photo opportunity in as many minutes.

"I'm sorry," he said, as yet another stranger called him by name as we walked past. "I honestly forgot about this."

We awaited the start of the parade on the sidewalk next to where Joe's float was parked, roughly halfway back from the Dykes on Bikes (the traditional parade openers), along with the two other scantily attired, extravagantly muscled young men who were to ride the float along with Joe: an obsidian-black boy with an eight-pack of abs and a waist I probably could have encircled with my fingers, though I imagined he had a price list for various bodily touchings, and a Latino with large silver rings through his pierced Hershey's Kiss nipples and an ass like two sofa cushions; they were a homoerotic Rainbow coalition. I leaned my (much older and, I concede, considerably less impressive) ass against a nearby parking meter; by now, I was pretty much used to the flesh-hungry glances of passersby (few-to-none directed at me, please note) and suitably smug about the fact that Joe remained epoxied to my side, his thumb hooked to the belt-loop at the back of my Levi's, as he nodded a greeting or acknowledged a shout-out with a smile and eyebrow-flash.

Suddenly, Joe said, "Oh, shit." He was staring down the street, his face taking on the look of a small animal seriously contemplating chewing through its own foot.

"What?" I glanced in the same direction and saw neither Godzilla stomping the Rage bar to splinters, nor the Ku Klux Klan stampeding down Santa Monica Boulevard on horseback. Then I noticed a tall lean man in what looked like a black leather tennis skirt, making his long-striding way toward us. He waved a long arm (exposing a pale, smoothly shaven armpit) and shouted, "Yo, Joey!"

Joe said, "Walk with me," and grabbed my hand and started down the street away from Skirt Guy at a pace just shy of racewalking, leaving me little choice but to walk, and walk quickly. I had just opened my mouth to ask what the Sam Hill was going on, when Joe said, "Did you see that guy?"

"Skirt Guy?"

Joe nodded. "He used to be my—"

"Boyfriend?" I interrupted.

We hot-footed an entire city block before Joe said, "Dealer," and maneuvered us behind the side of a large vintage fire engine and stopped. Standing so close to me that in almost any other circumstance, it would have been a prelude to sex, Joe leaned in and spit words out like watermelon seeds, "I was a crystal addict. For a couple of years. I'm not using anymore, okay? I swear."

"Okay," I said, taken more than slightly aback by the wildness in Joe's eyes. I had read about crystal meth (actually, one could scarcely pick up a gay-oriented newspaper or magazine without reading about it), and I knew from such reading that its abuse was a blight on the gay community and was being held responsible for a spike in new HIV infections. I barely had time to wonder if Joe had been high on crystal when he got infected, when he said, "I can't be around guys who are using and guys I knew when I was using. I can't. I can't. I can't." He'd broken a sweat and he was shaking his head no, over and over.

I took his face in my hands and said, "Okay, baby, it's okay," though I wasn't particularly sure it was okay at all.

I heard somebody say, "Joey!" and Joe jumped—I swear, he was actually airborne for a moment—as Skirt Guy approached, shirtless and sinewy and slightly out of breath. From this vantage point, I could see that he was no babe in arms (forty years old if he was an hour), and that he was wearing black eyeliner. In conjunction with the black leather tutu, it made for an ensemble that caused me to regret that the non-black gay community has no real equivalent for the phrase, "Niggah, please!"

"Whatcha running for, Joey?" he said, standing closer to my boyfriend than I found optimally comfortable and close enough for me to notice he had foam at the corners of his mouth. He seemed not to notice my existence, something which I had pretty much gotten used to.

Joe stepped back and to the side, half-hiding behind me as he said, "I told you, Frankie, I'm not doing that shit anymore." This Frankie person took a step forward, close enough for me to smell the funk coming off of the guy's sculpted chest.

"What shit is that, Joey?" he said. In full-on close-up, I could see that the guy might have been handsome in an angular sort of way, but his cheeks, chin, and forehead were marred with ruddy eruptions worse than any case of acne I'd ever seen. He shrugged broad, bony shoulders and said, "I just wanted to hang with you, that's all."

Joe shouted loud enough to make my ears ring, "I can't hang with you, Frankie. I told you. Now, leave me alone."

The guy moved in closer—one of the couple of the sores on his forehead was seeping. He said, "Come on, dude," his voice deep and low, like a character in a porn video trying to get his "straight" buddy to agree to a bit of dude-on-dude action.

Then somebody said, in a testosterone-laced voice I didn't quite recognize, "He said go away." Frankie turned and looked in my face for the first time, and I realized *I* had said it.

He said, "I wasn't talkin' to you, bitch," and turned back to Joe.

I did my best to remember where I'd pulled that voice from and used it to say, "Get the fuck away from him," loudly and with feeling.

It was enough to make Frankie retreat a couple of steps. He looked back at me and I took the opportunity to expand my white-T-shirted chest to its full depth and clench my back teeth to make my jaw jut out. It was about as manly a look as I figured I could muster, especially considering this Frankie guy was a full head taller than I was.

Frankie cocked his long head to one side, taking visual stock of me in my manliest stance. After a moment, a nasty-looking one-sided smile curled his lips. I'd seen that smile before: it was the smile of Michael Ponciano, who had regularly relieved me of my lunch money in the fourth grade; it was the smile of Scott Bengston, who had called me a fag in front of a playground full of kids in the sixth; it was the smile of every schoolyard bully from the beginning of recorded history—and I'd seen more than my fair share. Frankie stepped toward me, swaggering about as well as a man wearing a skirt (even a black leather skirt) can swagger, stopped nearly nose-to-nose with me, and said, "Who's gonna make me?" Then he poked me hard in the sternum with a long index finger. "You?"

Just FYI: I really, but *really* hate being poked in the chest. By anybody. It's just one of those things that really makes my ass pucker. "Quit that!" I said, briefly forgetting about the whole manly voice thing and hitting a high tenor note.

"What?" he said, and poked me again. And again he said, "What?" And then again with the poking.

And I don't know what came over me (maybe it was the Tribulus and Long Jack supplement I'd been taking in the hopes of "optimizing testosterone," as it said on the bottle) or what old Jimmy Cagney movie I suddenly thought I was starring in, but the next thing I knew, there's this sound, sort of a crack-splat, and Frankie's nose was spurting blood all over his lips. He screamed like Fay Wray in King

Kong's fist, reached up and wiped the fingertips of both hands in the bloody snot on his face, stared in wide wonder at his fingers, and then screamed again.

"You bitch!" he shouted, then looked at his red-painted hands again and added, "You nigger bitch!" He walked backward a couple of steps, accidentally colliding with a seven-foot Sister of Perpetual Indulgence (a veritable float all by herself, all tulle and glitter in homemade Flying Nun headgear), then turned and jogged away, up the Boulevard, covering his face with both hands and blubbering further malediction in my general direction.

I began to tremble as if experiencing a sudden cold snap. From the pounding in my chest and temples, my blood pressure must have been through the roof. I suddenly realized my hand hurt, as did my shoulder. I had never punched a grown man in my life, and pretty much considered fisticuffs to be the last desperate resort of the terminally dull-witted. I briefly thought I might cry.

I turned to Joe, who looked at me with an expression I couldn't begin to read.

"I'm sorry," I said. "I'm ... I'm not a hitter."

Joe took my face into his hands and kissed me softly on the lips, just barely slipping me some tongue on the way out (during which I'm pretty sure I heard someone walking by say, "*Mmm*, could I get some of that?"). Then he wrapped his arms around me and leaned into my ear to whisper, "Thank you, Daddy." Then he kissed my face and said, "Come on, I've got to get back to that fuckin' float." He took me by the hand and we started back.

And between my extreme self-disappointment at having resorted to physical violence and the swelling in my jeans that had me walking like an old cowboy, I couldn't remember when I'd been quite so conflicted. On top of which, much of the right side of my body had begun to throb, and I realized I may well have seriously injured my hand. My shoulder. And possibly my back.

7.

June gave way to July, as she must. And then came August, and the cusp of autumn. And Hurricane Katrina. I was at the Sullivans' in the midst of a Friday evening Dominoes tourney, when Maggie asked me, "Are any of your relatives affected by the hurricane?" Maggie was sitting opposite Joe, who was a last-minute sub for her husband, who was working late—the varnish wasn't dry on some big deal—and I was partnered with Ethan, whose new haircut (a West Hollywood version of a Marine Corps high-and-tight) had rendered him hotter than ever. A CD I'd burned for Ethan was playing over the stereo system: Beyoncé was looking so crazy over the rhythm track from "Family Affair" by Sly and the Family Stone—one of my favorite mash-ups, "Crazy Love Affair." The joy of being crazy in love with Joe Callahan was nearly matched by the joy of introducing a teenager to mash-up culture.

I asked Maggie, "What hurricane is that, my dear?" as I peered into Ethan's face, trying to read his expression. It was his turn to play, but instead of looking at his tiles, Ethan was staring, rather intently I thought, at Joe. "You can't have him," I said to Ethan.

"What?" Ethan started as if awakened from a nap. I wondered if Maggie had noticed Ethan's odd mood. He had emailed me earlier that same day to let me know that his Internet boyfriend had turned out to be a phony—he'd apparently admitted to having posted photos of some other guy and claimed they were him. *pls don't say I told u so*, Ethan had typed. *What would be the fun in that?* I'd replied. As it turns out, all this hard-won world wisdom that comes with age is a sour sort of gift—an expensive silk necktie in a color you hate. The young never listen to the old—they have to learn from their own mistakes—so there you sit on your middle-aged ass and your goddamn wisdom.

"Hello?" Maggie fairly shouted.

"What?"

"Hurricane *Katrina*," Maggie said. "What planet are you on?"

"You can stare at Callahan all you want," I said to Ethan, "but he's mine." Ethan blushed a strawberry scarlet. And then I said to Maggie, "You know, I've stopped watching the news. It depresses me." Which was true. I'd recently taken to ignoring even the headlines on the LCD screens in the office elevators. Between friends dropping left, right, and center all through the spring and Clara's continued illness, my threshold for bad news—never particularly high—was all but nonexistent.

"Johnnie," Maggie said in a voice whiny with concern, "Louisiana has been devastated. And Mississippi. New Orleans is under water. Don't you have family there?"

I felt the blood leave my face. "In St. Charles," I said. "And Slidell."

I took a quick look around me for my cell phone.

Joe put a hand to my arm and said, "It's in your jacket by the door."

I pushed myself up, did a quickstep to the entryway, and sat in the pew; dug my cell out of my Levi's jacket pocket, flipped it open, and said, "Mom."

Daniel answered on the fifth or sixth ring. He said, "Hey, John." Before I could ask, he added, "Clara's sleeping. She's been so worried about Theo, she hasn't been sleeping well. So when she does get to sleep, I don't disturb her."

"What about Theo?" I asked. My aunt Theo, Mom's kid sister (and last surviving sibling), had been institutionalized for Alzheimer's two, maybe three years before, somewhere in Louisiana, I wasn't sure where.

My aunt Theodosia had been one of the most remarkable-looking women I'd ever met, running a close second to her big sister, my mother. Statuesque where Clara was petite, Theo had legs that may well have gone clear up to her neck, had they not been stopped by a pair of the most amazing, all natural gazongas the world has ever seen. A cheerleader in high school, she'd become a personal trainer in her forties, after marrying, bearing a son (my cousin Walter, currently serving twenty-five-to-life for a gang-related killing), divorcing, and (wait for it) curing her own breast cancer through macrobiotics and Eastern alternative medicine. But when Theo's short-term memory began to flake away like old house paint on aluminum siding, nothing helped: neither Eastern medicine nor Western, prayer, wishful thinking, or voodoo.

"Her nursing home was evacuated," he said. "We don't know where she is. You can't get any calls through. And Clara's ..." He trailed off and there was just his breathing for what seemed like a long while.

"Daniel, what?" I was simultaneously aware that my left hand was clenched into a fist so tight it was cramping and that Joe was standing next to me. He squeezed the back of my neck with his small but well-padded hand.

"The headaches are back, John. I'm afraid the tumor is growing again." I heard myself whisper "fuck," then felt Joe's fingers kneading the back of my neck. I waited for the eviscerating imp to arrive, but Joe must have scared it away.

"I'm coming over," I said. "Tonight." I hadn't seen Clara in two weekends. I'd gotten complacent and lazy, and now her tumor was growing, and her sister (whose mind was all but obliterated by disease) was God-only-knew-where, and the place my mother still (inexplicably) called Home was all but washed away; and while I was neither so naïve nor so conceited as to assume a causal correlation, I knew I had to get to her. "You don't need to wait up. I can let myself in."

"I'll wait," he said. Daniel always waited, always opened the huge front door for me, no matter what time I arrived. Like Erich von Stroheim in *Sunset Boulevard*, lately Daniel seemed to live only to serve his lady. I flipped the phone shut, leaned back against Joe's hand, and said, "I've got to go to the desert, see my mom."

Joe said, "I'll go with you."

"No need," I said, pushing myself up from the bench, feeling old and weary and in need of all the moral support I could get.

Joe turned to face me. "I wasn't asking," he said. The lump in the middle of my chest pushed tears up into my eyes. I kissed my Joe's lips. Then I noticed Ethan, standing just behind Joe (a full head taller and peering at me over Joe's shoulder), the look on his face as inscrutable as the Cyrillic alphabet.

Marjorie Fair was singing "fill my empty room with the sun" from the in-wall speakers as I made my apologies to Maggie, who hugged me hard and made the appropriate sounds of sympathy and encouragement. Joe was out the front door and halfway to the car with my keys jingling like Christmas bells in his hand when I held my arms out for a hug from Ethan. All at once, Ethan took my face into his long hands and kissed me: first his lips (prickly with his recent attempt at a mustache) and then his tongue, spicy from the chips and salsa we'd been munching. A little grunt escaped Ethan's mouth and into my own as his tongue swept across my gums. Then he let go of me, turned heel, and longstepped his way down the hall to his room without a word.

From the sheer surprise, my general state of emotional upheaval, and the fact that young Ethan had proved to be quite the kisser, I stood a bit unsteady on my feet for a moment. I called good night to no one in particular (I was quite alone) and walked out to the car, pulling the front door shut behind me. This would require some processing. Fortunately, I had a two-hour drive ahead.

Daniel met us at the door after a full minute of my ringing and knocking—I was just about to use my key. It was August in Palm Desert, eighty-something degrees at nearly midnight, and Daniel was apparently fresh from the pool: a huge white towel sarong'd around his waist, and his head, chest hair, and (since I'd last seen him) new full beard was visibly damp. He looked like the cover of some triple-X DVD called *Daddy Bears Gone Wild* or something. Or maybe it was just me.

I introduced Daniel to Joe ("Joe Callahan, this is my mother's husband"), somewhat hesitantly describing Joe as my boyfriend (a term that, for reasons I would have to sort out later, I found difficult to utter in front of Daniel Weinberger). Daniel said, "Pleasure to meet you," and clasped Joe's hand with no discernible signs of disapproval.

I heard Clara's voice, lilting nearly to the point of song, "And when do *I* get introduced?" she said, making her barefoot way toward the door as Daniel shut it behind us. Clara approached Joe, arms extended in greeting, passing me by as if I were a doorstop. In denim shorts and one of Daniel's oversize V-neck T-shirts, her (recently returned, very short) hair cornrowed into swirls that reminded me of Van Gogh's *Starry Night*, Clara looked a bit thinner than I'd last seen her and somehow more beautiful—fine and delicate as filigree. "I'm Johnnie's mother," she said, taking Joe's face into her hands. A blush rose in Joe's café-au-lait cheeks and he smiled with every tooth in his head, smiled so big his eyes narrowed.

"Mother," I said as if she had acknowledged my existence, "this is Joe Callahan. Joe, this is the legendary Clara Johnson Rousseau Weinberger." I caught a glimpse of my mother's husband retreating toward the bedrooms.

"Come on in," Clara said, taking my hand in hers and slipping her other arm around Joe's. "I put on some coffee," she said, leading us to the kitchen. "Would you like some coffee, Joe?" Then she squeezed my hand with an amazing amount of strength for one so small and said, "It's about time."

"How do you take it, Joe?" she asked, pouring. At some point, Clara had read that saying the name of someone you've just met three times helped cement it in your mind, and she'd been doing it ever since. She had one more to go. Joe took it black. She handed him the steaming mug, saying, "Careful, Joe—that's very hot." She smiled, undoubtedly satisfied she would never forget Joe's name, and then asked, "How old are you, Joe? You look like a baby."

Joe was blowing into his coffee cup, the luscious moue of his lips suggestive of so many things that I nearly forgot my own name. "I'm thirty-one, ma'am."

Never a slouch in arithmetic, Clara looked at me with eyes filled to the brim with meaning. "Seventeen years younger than Johnnie." It had actually not occurred to me that my lover was the same number of years younger as my mother's husband was. In any case, the degree to which I have *become* my mother can sometimes astonish, and somewhat disturb me.

Clara and I sat half-sunken into the warm leather of the family room sofa; Clara was sipping kettle coffee as Joe sat cross-legged on the floor in front of her, rubbing her feet. She'd actually *asked* him to, I swear—on something like fifteen minutes' acquaintance, she suddenly said, "Joe-baby, would you rub my feet, please."

She blew a steam cloud across the top of her coffee mug, took a slurpy sip, and then said, "We still don't know where Theo is." She spoke softly, looking into her coffee. "I assume somewhere in Texas, but we can't get any calls through." Then she slightly bent her right leg, disengaging her foot from Joe's hands. "Thank you, baby," she said. "That was nice." Joe slid on his blue-jeaned ass away from Clara and parked between my feet, the back of his head at my groin. I reached over and stroked the side of Joe's neck, just reflex: if Joe was within arm's length, I wanted my hands on him.

"I'm happy you're seeing somebody," Clara said. She leaned her head back against the sofa. "Life is short." I wasn't sure if she was deliberately opening up a discussion of her worsening health, but I wasn't feeling quite up to it just then. I just said, "*Hmm.*"

I turned to Clara, meaning to suggest we all go to bed, when I noticed my mother's fingers loosen on the mug she was holding and

I reached over to catch it before she let go. The slow, even breath escaping her parted lips cued me that she had fallen asleep. I used Joe's bulky shoulder to help push myself up from the sofa, and would have set off to find Daniel, but suddenly he was there, as if he had somehow heard his wife's eyelids fall shut.

"The guest room's all ready for you," he whispered, and then scooped Clara up into his arms as if she were a small child. She leaned against Daniel's chest, her face tucked into her husband's neck, and a sleepy little sound rose from her throat. Daniel whispered good night, and was down the hall, carrying one small, sick lady to her bed.

I took Joe's hand and led him toward ours.

Joe and I slept until nearly seven, then we lingered almost an hour, wrapped around one another, Joe slowly humping against my thigh— no goal in mind, just rubbing. I'd learned pretty early on that while Joe truly liked sex (and truly liked sex with *me*), much of the time he preferred to cuddle. Like the girl in "Love for Sale," he'd been through the mill of love: he'd had at least his fair share of sex—for love, for fun, for free, for pay, and at least once (at the tender age of fourteen) for a burger, fries, and a large Coke; in private and public, in print, on film, and (at a particularly festive New York City circuit party in the late 1990s) live onstage. Given the choice, he'd nearly always choose a hug over a fuck. True, this particular cuddle party did end with Joe sucking me so doggone good I nearly bit a pillow in half, then jerking a ribbon of spooge from my nuts to my nose.

Once showered and dressed (overdressed, really, for Palm Desert in the summer—jeans and T-shirts, barefoot), we made our way to the kitchen, which was deserted. I had just located the filters for the space shuttle Clara called a coffee maker when Daniel and Clara entered the kitchen, Clara tucked under her husband's furry arm, looking like one large, lumpy four-legged black-and-white monster from *Star Trek*. Clara was wearing one of her Afro-print dashiki dresses with a matching bandana tied around her head. She smiled upon seeing me, the dimples in her cheeks looking deep as a Bergman film.

"Baby," she said, "when did you get here?" Daniel whispered something that might have been "Honey," and then Clara noticed Joe perched on a stool at the kitchen counter. "I'm Clara," she said. "Johnnie's mother." Joe looked back at me, eyebrows high on his face. Daniel leaned down to whisper into Clara's ear. Her smile faded and she laughed a little cough of a laugh.

"I'm sorry," she said to me, or Joe, or the kitchen counter. "This," and she looked up and blinked rapidly a few times; a tear fell anyway, and she pushed at it with the heel of her hand, "happens sometimes."

I looked at Daniel's face. I wish I could describe the look on that big, open, nose-burdened face, but it told me Daniel would have given his everlasting soul to keep this from "happening" to his wife.

"Probably end up like my sister," Clara said, words coming fast and high. "Last time I saw her, she didn't know anybody, not even me. I keep asking Daniel to smother me in my sleep with a pillow, but he just won't do it." She wriggled free of Daniel and started toward me. I had been holding a scoop of finely ground Costa Rican coffee poised in mid-air for what may have been years. "You gonna make some coffee, baby?"

She stopped at Joe and, with an odd, almost flirtatious smile, said to him, "I realize I'm supposed to know, but—"

"I'm Joe," he said.

"Joe," Clara repeated, reaching up to touch Joe's face, softly with her fingertips. "Joe. Joe. I won't forget again."

We spent a quiet day. Far too hot to consider venturing outdoors (even the swimming pool was useless—it would have felt like bath water), we mostly sat on the family room sofa (in the blessed air conditioning) and watched movies: Clara, Joe, and me. Clara wanted to see *National Lampoon's Christmas Vacation* again and shot me a "Wanna make something of it?" look as she took the DVD out of its case. Clara and I laughed at all the same *schtick* we'd laughed at in May and Joe had the remarkable good taste not to question our Christmas in August.

Joe made piled-high turkey sandwiches for lunch, which we ate while watching Ray Charles in concert; in spite of my urgings, Clara only picked a little piece of turkey out of her sandwich and shoved the rest away.

We didn't talk about the cancer. It just hung there over our heads all day, like a piñata full of poison.

Finally, near the end of the show, during "America the Beautiful," Clara suddenly took my hand and said, "Don't be angry with God." I turned to look at my mother's face, which for some reason, for the very first time I could recall, looked every day of her age. Her Native American cheekbones seemed about to pierce through her skin and dark shadows surrounded her almond eyes. "I was, for awhile," she continued. "First Theo and that Alzheimer's, and now this," she managed to indicate the monster growing beneath her skull with one tilt of her head. She squeezed my hand. "But I'm not angry anymore. And don't you be, either. It's like a weight on your heart, being mad at God." She turned back to the obscenely large video screen, where Ray, The Raelettes, a gospel choir, and a good-sized orchestra were heading for the big finish, the closing credits scrolling across Ray's face.

I saw no point in going into a theological discussion with my terminally ill mother. The fact was, I had long before ceased believing in the kind of God I could get angry with, that big white-bearded amalgam of Santa Claus, a Vegas slot machine, and my late father who could choose to reward good works or not and could choose to punish for no good reason. As beliefs go, this one struck me as primitive and a bit childish. (Though if it works for you, by all means, go with it.) Even as I handed out communion wafers to trannies and leather daddies at Temple of Love, even as I had laid hands and prayed for my own mother's healing, I certainly didn't believe that some big guy in the sky was scratching his big fat head, deciding whether or not to allow my very nearly septuagenarian mother a few more years or a few more weeks on earth. I was still in the process of sorting out what it was I *did* believe about prayer and healing, but I knew I didn't believe that. But to say that to Clara, Butterfly McQueen bandana wrapped around her cancer-riddled head, and the ghost of the late Brother Ray hugging himself and grinning to his last molar, would have seemed condescending and mean-spirited. So I simply squeezed her small, warm hand back and said, "I'm not angry."

Clara smiled, slipped her hand from mine and said, "I'm tired. I'm gonna rest awhile." And as if he had learned to read Clara's thoughts (and who knows, maybe he had), Daniel was suddenly there, the impressive bulk of his legs on display in khaki walking shorts. "Exactly what I was about to suggest," he said. And Clara tucked herself beneath his arm, one puzzle piece against its mate.

Joe and I were both in full squat, picking up crumb-littered paper plates and napkins from the floor, when Daniel returned.

"John," he said, "you and Joe should be getting back home." I was being dismissed again. I turned and gave him a look meant to simulate one of those sassy plus-size black actresses on one of those sitcoms starring some minor rap artist, where people say things like "No she *dih-ent!*" I opened my mouth to protest, then thought better of it. Clara had probably asked him to dismiss me. And even if she hadn't, he was, after all, her husband. "You know she loves to see you," he continued, "but having company really takes it out of her." Daniel took the used paper goods from my hand and adjourned to the kitchen.

I turned to Joe and said, "Well, I guess it's time to go." We packed our respective toothbrushes into our respective gym bags and let ourselves out. Joe volunteered to drive again, and again, I let him.

We had scarcely cleared the driveway when a pain stabbed my right nut like some berserk Rockette's kick to the groin, so hard and so sudden I jackknifed from the waist and bumped my head on the sun visor. I screamed, "Shit!" once when Trixie's dancing shoe slammed my ball, and again when my forehead slammed the Honda's interior. Joe hit the brake.

"Honey!" he said, like somebody's exasperated wife. I turned to spot Joe's face broadcasting disapproval. "*Now* will you please call the HMO?"

I leaned back hard against the car seat with the pain in my crotch and the pain in my forehead pounding counterpoint. "Yes," I said. "I'll call them."

8.

I won't go into an extended *schtick* about how I hate my HMO because (let's face it) nobody *likes* their HMO. I'll just let it suffice to say that, in order to get a second opinion on my recurring severe ball-ache, I first had to make an appointment to see my primary care physician—who would very likely do absolutely nothing. Not that seeing my primary care physician is such a hardship, since (as I may have mentioned) my primary care physician—one Sasan Maradifar—is a five-star babe. Still, it doesn't strike me as the most efficient way of doing things. But I did as I was told, like a good boy. And the good news was I only had to wait one day to get in to see Sasan.

I arrived at the HMO's offices the suggested fifteen minutes early for my ten a.m. appointment and sat in the waiting room reading a fifteen-month-old issue of *AARP* magazine until 10:20, when the nurse (a tall rawboned thing with a glaringly artificial short stack of curls pinned to the top of her head, like a Denny's waitress) shouted out my name, led me backstage, and took my temperature (98.7— I've always run a temp that is a bit warm) and my blood pressure (127 over 77, which she assured me was very good), weighed me (166 with all my clothes on), and ushered me into an exam room with the promise that the doctor would be in "momentarily."

As just about everyone knows, doctors are like Jehovah, to the extent that to them, a day is as a hundred years and a hundred years as a day. I perched on the exam table and, assuming a long sit, decided to read the various posters, charts, and flyers nailed, stapled, and thumbtacked to the walls. My gaze had just stopped upon a brightly colored cross-section of the male genitalia (reminding me of a Georgia O'Keefe painting) when Sasan entered.

"How are you?" he asked through an Aquafresh smile, his right hand extended. I shook his hand (solid but well-cushioned, like an expensive sofa) and gave my traditional retort, "If I were *well*, I wouldn't be here, now would I?" And added, "Not that it isn't always a pleasure to see you." I wasn't jivin'—if you're going to have your nads fondled by a man with no intention of ever slurping your sausage, that man may as well be Dr Maradifar.

"So," he said, settling into the room's only chair, "what brings you here today?"

I considered reminding him that a glance at the clipboard he was holding would probably give him a clue, but thought better of it and said, in as deadpan a voice as I could muster, "My balls hurt."

Sasan's long-lashed eyes met my own. "Still?"

"Again," I said. "Off and on for over a year. And as you're unlikely to recall, the biblically ancient urologist I spoke to six months ago told me he had no idea why my balls hurt, that it would probably go away eventually, and if not, I should take an aspirin when the pain got to be too much. Oh, yes. He did mention that I should get used to a certain amount of physical discomfort because, quote—You're at that age—end of quote. Well, it's been a year, it has decidedly *not* gone away, and I'd like to see if someone else might come up with something a bit more helpful than 'take an aspirin.'"

Sasan crossed his legs at the knee (causing me to take notice of his beautiful black tasseled loafers) before saying, "So you'd like a second opinion."

I leaned slightly forward, looking directly into Dr M's Bambi eyes. "Sasan," I said, slowly and deliberately, as if addressing a small child with learning issues, "my balls hurt. For a year. *You* have balls. Would you like your balls to hurt for a year?" I fought the urge to add, "I could *arrange* that, you know."

"Ah," he said, as if that actually meant something, and scribbled something onto the uppermost sheet of paper on his clipboard. "I will contact the Urology Department. They should be contacting you in the next day or two." He extended his right hand again: doctor body language for "time's up." Not so much as a quick fondle. "Maybe a younger urologist," he added as he nodded to the open door. As his hand landed between my shoulder blades—something between a pat and a gentle nudge out the door—he added, "I can't make you any promises, of course. I'm afraid you'll find that sometimes things just hurt, for no good reason. Fact is, you *are* at that age." And I was facing the Exit sign before I had a chance to suggest to my über-cute primary care physician that he might kiss my *entire* middle-aged black ass.

The HMO being the HMO, I assumed I'd be a considerably older man by the time they got back to me with an appointment. To my shock, there was a voice message for me from the HMO by the time I got back to work. Dr Goldfarb would see me the very next morning at ten.

I arrived at the Urology Department of the HMO at a quarter of ten, used my debit card for the fifteen-dollar co-pay, and settled into the plastic-upholstered waiting room chair. I'd brought the current *Out* magazine with me (I subscribe—there was this really cute boy trying to earn a trip to Punta Cana by selling magazine subscriptions, what can I tell you?), and I flipped through the pages as I waited. There was a Dolce & Gabbana underwear ad so nearly pornographic I accidentally tore off a corner flipping the page, hoping neither of the octogenarians sitting near me in the waiting room saw it.

I slowed down at a fashion layout called "Look Sharp at Any Age." The first double-page spread was subtitled "20s," the next "30s," and then "40s"; each featuring one or more handsome, taut-muscled examples of Anglo-American manhood modeling attire deemed appropriate to the corresponding age group. I turned the page, in hopeful expectation of the "50s" spread, but instead found an article on Gay Mardi Gras in Sydney: apparently, after forty-nine, fashion suddenly ceases to matter. Presumably, nobody much cares what a Troll is wearing, since nobody wants him anyhow. No way was *Out* going to feature the official Auntie uniform (Hawaiian print shirts and khaki Sansabelt trousers), and a true Daddy wears anything he fuckin' *wants*, Boy.

I was mentally composing a snippy letter to the editor, when an Asian-looking nurse roughly the size of the average fourth grader (sporting a mushroom-cap haircut that made me think of the poison-blowdart-wielding South Sea Islanders in *Raiders of the Lost Ark*) opened the door and shouted my name into the clipboard she carried.

I followed her into a large, white, unflatteringly lit room somewhat overfull of apparatus reminding me of Colin Clive's laboratory from *The Bride of Frankenstein*. Nurse tossed a folded hospital gown at my knees (I had to crouch to catch it) and said, "Take off you clothes, gown open in back, lie down on table, I come back." Or something to that effect. I felt a chill not entirely attributable to the apparent lack of heating in the room as I kicked off my Sperry Top-Siders, pulled my not-quite-a-Lacoste polo shirt over my head, and lowered my relaxed-fit jeans.

I lay on the table in only the backless flannel frock and my socks, counting the holes in the acoustic ceiling tiles directly over my head, when Nurse returned, her crêpe soles squeaking on the floor.

"I going to clean you," she said, and flipped the hem of my gown up to my chest. Before I could so much as look down, she was pouring what felt like a gallon of ice-water over my naked genitals. My entire body went to gooseflesh and I sang a long, upward glissando to what may have been a soprano high E-flat (a nearby glass beaker may have shattered, I'm not sure). Before my clacking jaws were able to form the F-word, my peripheral vision caught Nurse's crisp white back heading toward the door. Over the sound of my own gasping breaths, I heard her say, "Doctor be with you minute." Or something to that effect.

Like the bedroom door in a French farce, the exam room door had scarcely closed behind Nurse Wretched before it swung open again and a short, redheaded, lab-coated young man strode into the room. He said, "Good morning, I'm Dr Goldfarb," without actually glancing down at me and immediately began raising a clatter with some sort of instruments on a metal tray on a table across the room.

I raised myself up on my elbows and took a better look at Dr Goldfarb who, as it turned out, bore a cousin-like resemblance to my former analyst (redheaded and liberally freckled, Howdy Doody in a lab coat). Exposed, chilled, and damp, I mustered what little of my scattered dignity I could find and asked, "How old are you, Dr Goldfarb?"

"I'm thirty-four," he said without looking up, and continued the clatter.

"And exactly what are we going to be doing today, Dr Goldfarb?" If I've been told once, I've been told a dozen times (generally by friends with HIV or AIDS) that doctors will usually tell you absolutely jack-shit-nothing unless you ask. I had recently been advised to always ask doctors what they intend to do, since it was not unheard of for them to walk in with someone else's chart and/or their very own head up their very own ass. This advice had most recently come from a friend of mine who had been overdosed on an anticoagulant meant for another patient, and ended up with a blood bubble the size of a volleyball growing out of the right side of his abdomen.

"Well," said Dr G., finally turning to face me, "we're going to take a look at your bladder, your prostate, and your seminal vesicles." The doc held in one hand what looked to my untrained layperson's eye to be a two-foot length of gently curving surgical steel tubing, diameter roughly halfway between a paper clip and number-two Ticonderoga pencil. He pointed to the end of the tube and said, "There's a camera right here, see?"

"And exactly how are we going to get the camera to see my bladder?" The question had barely escaped my still-trembling lips before I knew exactly how and, if possible, my blood ran colder. I closed my eyes and clenched my teeth as Dr Goldfarb replied,

"I'm going to insert this into your penis." I briefly considered leaping from the table and running for the door, but as I was nearly naked and quite wet, that seemed unlikely. "Possible complications," he continued, "include urethral infection. And you may find some blood in your urine for a few days."

Picnic in the freakin' park, I thought. "And how much is this little procedure likely to hurt?" I asked as Dr Goldfarb approached my table, the hideous metallic thing in his hands seeming to lengthen exponentially as he walked forward.

A smile dallied in the corners of his thin lips. With a hand to my shoulder, he gently but firmly encouraged me to lie back.

"Not much," he said. "Not much at all."

Liar. Liar. Pants on muthafuckin' fire.

In the movie *In & Out*, starring Kevin Kline as the recently "outed" gay small-town schoolteacher, one of Kevin's students (a football jock) explains the unnaturalness of homosexuality by pointing out that the human body includes "in" holes (i.e., the mouth) and "out" holes (specifically, the anus). Before my introduction to Dr Goldfarb (and his introduction of the Piston of Pain to my privates), I had simply chuckled at this movie character's rather naïve brand of anatomy-based homophobia. But now I know better, and I am passing my new-found wisdom on to you, just FYI:

The urethra is an "out" hole. It is absolutely *not* an "in" hole. And yes, I realize that you may be one of those erotically adventurous types, given to adventurous sex play with things like catheters and sounds, blithely pushing and pulling foreign objects in and out of your pee-pee-hole, just for funzies. And if you are one of those types, I have this to say to you: Whaddaya, crazy?!? If you are not one of those people, heed these words, write them in hemorrhage-red ink in today's page of your mental diary: If anyone ever says to you, "I am going to insert this into your penis"—run. Run as fast as you can. Hesitate only long enough to jab this person in the eye with something sharp, should he or she attempt to pursue you. If no such sharp object is readily available, just run faster. This has been a public service announcement.

The clean white walls of the exam room echoed with my screams as the cold steel slowly entered my little "out" hole. I yelled a steady, non-stop siren as Dr Goldfarb (a criminally insane version of Opie Taylor in a white jacket) shoved the camera-wielding rod up the length of my penis, then gasped a breath and screamed anew as the cold, hard intruder poked through my pelvic sphincter (I could have sworn I heard a popping sound, even over the sound of my own screaming). The doctor repeated "Try to relax"—an easy enough request, I imagine, if one does not have a camera up one's cock, but quite out of the question for me under the circumstances. My entire body became a fist. Days, perhaps weeks later, I sang my entire two-and-a-half octave range as the doctor pulled the tube out of me in one long, steady motion.

Once my body was finally free of Dr G.'s implement of torture, I pushed myself up to a seated position and shouted at full vocal capacity,

"Fuck you! Fuck your mama! Fuck your whole fuckin' family!" And for good measure, I added, "Fucker!" I mostly shouted it to Dr Goldfarb's white-lab-coated back as he left the room. Nurse entered as doctor departed.

"Pick up you clothes," she said, "come other room." Or something to that effect. I looked down at my own battered genitals (half expecting to find my penis in tatters, like an Oscar Mayer wiener left in the boiling water too long) and found the paper beneath my naked ass covered with drying brown liquid. I must have gasped aloud as the possible identity of this substance (not to mention its possible origin) began occurring to me, because Nurse made a disapproving clicking noise with her tongue (as if she would have called me a big pussygirl if she'd only known of the term), rolled her almond eyes, and said, "It just iodine."

Somehow, I conquered the urge to murder this small unpleasant woman with my bare hands, and then gathered my clothes and followed her across the hall and into a second exam room.

Even considering that my aft orifice had considerably more past experience with intruders (organic or otherwise) than my fore, having a Magic Marker-sized camera introduced into my rectum was (to say the very least) no picnic. Tucked into the fetal position on yet another paper-covered exam table while Dr Doom adjusted and re-adjusted the high-tech widget wedged up my ass (or, as the doctor called it, my "tushie"—as in, "I need you to lie in the fetal position with your tushie out"—just too, too Jewish), I very nearly longed for the good old days of two feet of metal tubing up my dick. The device, and the good doctor's manipulations thereof, made for optimal I-could-poop-at-any-moment discomfort, without the slenderest hope of even the slightest prostate pleasure. Days, perhaps weeks later, he finally removed his kinky little sex toy from my "tushie" (making a sound not unlike the opening of a bottle of inexpensive Asti Spumanti), dropped a couple of heavy-duty paper towels onto the table near my clenched face, and said, "Okay, clean up, get dressed and meet me in my office."

Cleanup was the real challenge: Dr Goldfarb had been somewhat overzealous with the lube—I'd be farting K-Y jelly into my Jockeys for the rest of the day—and two quicker-picker-uppers proved woefully insufficient to the task.

I lowered myself carefully into one of Dr Goldfarb's guest chairs, once more fully clothed, feeling violated and skuzzy, desirous of a long hot shower, and prepared for the worst.

"Well," the doctor began, looking not so much at me as at an imaginary point just over my left shoulder, "I have good news and not-so-good news."

"Let's have the not-so-good," I said. "It's the way I am."

He shrugged a suit-yourself and said, "We still don't know why you're experiencing pelvic pain." Before I could begin shouting ("Muthafucka, you shoved a camera up my *dick*!"), he added, "But the good news is, your bladder is fine, your prostate is fine, and your seminal vesicles are fine. What you're experiencing may be referred pain from your abdominals or your quads. You obviously lift weights." He smiled a sheepish little excuse of a smile, as if slightly embarrassed to have noticed another man's musculature.

"Or," he said, "you may be developing a bit of arthritis in the lower back. Again, referred pain. And frankly," another thin-lipped little attempt at a smile, "you'll find more and more that things can ache for no good reason. You're at that age now."

It occurred to me that if I heard one more thirty-something MD telling me about how I'm "at that age," I would not be responsible for any physical damage I might inflict during the ensuing blackout.

"If the discomfort warrants it," he said, scribbling on a prescription pad, "feel free to take aspirin. Also," and he ripped the top sheet of paper free and handed it to me, "I suggest you take saw palmetto. It's herbal, you can get it at the pharmacy downstairs or at the health food store. Some men find it helps with pelvic pain." He folded his pale, freckled hands on the desk. I suddenly noticed that his fingernails seemed to have been gnawed to the scabby quick. "Do you have any questions?"

I took in a long, deep breath through my nostrils, blew it out slowly through my mouth, hoping to calm the desire to shriek like Janet Leigh in *Pscyho*. "Just so I'm clear," I said, as evenly as I could, "you've just shoved a camera up my piss-hole and another one up my shit-hole and you still don't know why my balls hurt."

"I'm afraid not," he said.

"And all you've got for me in terms of treatment is aspirin," I made a brief fanning motion with the prescription slip, "and something I can buy at Whole Foods."

Dr Goldfarb nodded. His lips parted as if he meant to say something—I suspect it was "You're at that age," and he had the good sense not to try that one again.

"Well, then," I said, pushing myself up from the chair, "I guess that's all she wrote, isn't it?" But I sat down again. "No," I said, "there's one more thing." He nodded permission. "Your nurse has the bedside manner of a Nazi war criminal."

Another one of those wan little smiles of his. "Sato can be a bit brusque," he said.

"Brusque?" I repeated. "I'm a relatively healthy man, Doctor; notwithstanding the chronically sore nuts. I'm pretty strong. I'm a *body*-builder, for cryin' out loud, and the bitch nearly reduced me to tears. I shudder to imagine what she must do to little old ladies."

"Are you suggesting I reprimand her?" he asked, absently pushing objects here and there on his desk. He was obviously finished with me and just wanted me out of his office.

"I suggest you have her committed to an institution for the criminally insane for the rest of her natural life. But I don't suppose that's going to happen, is it?" I pushed myself up from the chair, meaning it this time. "Well, thanks for"—(I found myself at a loss)—"whatever."

Oh, and just FYI: even if you've been forewarned, the first time you piss blood is, to say the least, disconcerting.

In spite of recurring discomfort south of my personal Mason-Dixon line, the rest of that week wasn't bad at all. *The Naked Truth* had ended its initial run, and Joe spent Monday through Thursday evenings with me; we watched the Ken Burns *Jazz* ten-DVD series over dinners we prepared together with tag-team precision, with Joe serving up his perfect body for dessert, and then we slept entangled all night—four consecutive days spent in Johnnie Heaven, only slightly marred by the knowledge that Joe had been hired to tend bar at The Abbey (West Hollywood's most popular bar, home of the most beautiful boys in the known universe and twenty-dollar apple martinis) for the entire weekend.

As a bonus, Harold Benjamin was on vacation, visiting relatives in Schenectady, leaving me with little to do at work than take the occasional phone message and transcribe them into emails to send to Harold (who, like most attorneys, lived with a Blackberry all but implanted on his hip). So if, for instance, my Wednesday morning commute was delayed by an hour or so due to a particularly lengthy good morning kiss, segueing into a particularly lengthy good morning fuck, *c'est la vie, c'est l'amour,* and believe you me, I regretted *rien.*

Come Friday morning, I was bored to near delirium and reduced to free-associating on the Internet—Google-searching for information on an obscure 70s rock band called Orchestra Luna, who had made one truly bizarre, utterly transcendent album, and then disbanded. (I'd bought the LP in high school, and had recently paid upwards of thirty bucks on Amazon for a Japanese import CD.) Across the double-wide cubicle, Vince was applying stickers bearing large, brightly colored client/matter file numbers onto blue pressboard file folders, exuding youthful sex appeal in a snug-fitting black T-shirt with a bright-red skull and crossbones across the chest. As was his habit, Vince offered up a non sequitur, by way of conversation: "I read where one of the guys on *That '70s Show* is into donkey-punching."

"I'm sure I'll be sorry," I said, "but what's donkey-punching?" I had Googled my way to pay dirt: a rather elaborate fan website dedicated to Orchestra Luna, where I'd already found several publicity shots of the band (lots of platform shoes and big big hair on both the guys and girls in the band), PDFs of the original album cover art, and a transcription of the song lyrics.

Vince barely looked up from his work, nor did he make any apparent attempt to lower his voice when he said, "It's where you're fucking a woman doggy-style—usually in the ass, but not necessarily—and just before you're gonna nut, you punch her real hard in the back of the head, which makes all her orifices tighten. To enhance your orgasm. Usually knocks the woman out cold." At which he turned to me and added, "I guess it'd work with a guy, too."

"I'll make a note of that," I said, when my cell phone rang from inside my center desk drawer (Clara's new ring tone: a plunking synthetic rendition of "Für Elise"—recently changed because, let's face it, Flavor Flav had been a bad idea). I pulled the drawer open and flipped the phone, expecting Clara's husband. "Daniel?"

"Not this time." It was Clara. I smiled at the sound of her voice. "You still coming out this weekend?"

"I planned to," I said. I'd left extra food and water for the cats and packed a gym bag and stowed it in the trunk of my car. "Is that okay?" I had a sneaking hunch she might ask me to stay away.

"It's fine, baby," she said. "I just wanted you to know I won't be at the house. I'm going in the hospital this afternoon."

All of my internal organs surged upward. "What?" I jumped up and quick-footed across the hall with the cell phone into Harold's office, locking the door behind me. I fell back into the softness of Harold's black leather sofa, closed my eyes, and braced myself for horror.

Clara said, "Calm yourself, now. It's not like that. They're just gonna take some tests. I'll spend one night there. That's it."

"That's it?" My heart was beating bass drum against my rib cage.

"That's it," she repeated in a tone that let me know she didn't much appreciate being challenged on the subject. "It's been planned for a week," she added. "I just forgot to mention it." I listened to my heart pounding in my ears for a moment. "The thing," Clara said, "the tumor, it's definitely stopped growing for awhile. Praise the Lord."

"Thank God." My heart rate slowed a bit.

"So come to the hospital," she said. "There's something I wanted to talk to you about."

"What is it?" The heart revved up again.

"Now, if I wanted to talk about it on the phone, I'd be doing it, wouldn't I?" When I couldn't come up with a retort, she added, "We'll talk when I see you."

I drove alone—Joe had bartending work. Friday evening traffic going out of town was even worse than its typical homicide-inducing horror, for no apparent reason. It took nearly three hours getting to the desert: my entire Joni playlist and most of Joan Armatrading. As I was passing Palm Springs on the I-10, crossing from Dante-esque desolation into palm-tree lined, man-made paradise, I speed-dialed Daniel's cell, and got his voice mail. It occurred to me that cell-phone use was likely prohibited in the hospital, so I flipped the phone shut without leaving a message. I'd just go on to the hospital and take my chances.

I felt a slight twinge of testicular pain just driving into the hospital parking lot, but I pressed on. I said hello to the weary-looking youngish Latina behind the front desk. When it became obvious that no return greeting was forthcoming, I said, "I'm here to see Clara Rousseau." I half expected her to send me on my way—surely, I thought, visiting hours must be over. But she simply tapped on the computer keyboard on the desk, eliciting a beep, and said, "What was that name again?"

I said, "Rousseau. Clara Rousseau." As the young woman began typing, I thought to correct myself: "I'm sorry. It's Weinberger. Clara Weinberger." She shot me a look, but then directed me toward a nearby bank of elevators and said, "Fourth floor."

Through the open doorway of the semiprivate room, I saw Clara reclining on top of the sheets, wearing one of her nicer housecoats (a quilted pale-pink number), white shorty socks on her feet, hands crossed over a tummy I didn't remember from the last time I'd seen her, staring up at the small television mounted on the opposite wall. I could hear the all-too-familiar voice of Pat Sajak inviting someone to buy a vowel. (*Jeopardy*, immediately followed by *Wheel of Fortune*, had been the linchpin of Clara's weekday evening routine for decades.) Daniel sat next to the bed, also intent on "*Wheel*" (as Clara called it), fairly spilling out of a metal chair that barely seemed capable of containing his muscular bulk—the same could be said for the baby-blue polo shirt and khaki shorts he wore.

I announced myself with a knock-knock on the doorjamb. Both Daniel and Clara turned. Daniel, ever the gentleman, pushed himself up from the chair (which I half-expected to find clinging to his ample khaki behind). Daniel and I did that day's variation on our habitual handshake/semi-hug tango, and as I bent to kiss my mother's upturned cheek, I realized how much fuller those cheeks were since last I saw them. Clara's face, full-moon round beneath a pink crocheted cloche, reminded me of pictures I'd seen of her in relative youth: pregnant with me, or shortly following my brother's birth, or with those white children she'd governessed back in the day (a day when, she had often confessed, she'd often treat herself to healthy helpings of vanilla ice cream before bedtime). My lips had barely made contact with Clara's smooth, cool face before she said, "I'm big as a house. This medication they've got me on."

"You're beautiful," I whispered, and I wasn't lying.

"Sit down, John," Daniel offered me his chair. "I'm going out for a breath of air," he said, starting for the door. His exit plan could not have been more apparent if he'd been carrying a script. "I'll be back in a little while," he said, then walked back to the bed and kissed Clara softly on the lips. And then he exited, stage left.

Clara looked toward the doorway for a moment, as if memorizing the sight of her husband's broad polo-shirted back. "He knows I want to talk to you alone," she said. She picked up the remote from her lap and turned off the television. "*Wheel*'s almost over," she said, as I sat in the chair abandoned by Daniel. Clara patted the bed beside her. "Come, sit up here." After briefly wondering how the medical staff might react to finding me perched in bed with my mother and quickly deciding I didn't give a tinker's dam, I kicked off my topsiders and climbed aboard, sitting cross-legged near the foot of the bed.

"Your roommate wasn't watching the show?" I asked. I'd noticed the tail end of a second bed and a pair of bedsheet-covered feet peeking out from behind the screen divider. Clara did a little shrug toward the screen.

"They gave Marge her meds a little bit ago. Couldn't wake her up with an atom bomb."

"Well, then, I guess she won't be eavesdropping."

"Not today," she said, her smile showing off the deep dimples in her newly rounded cheeks.

"So," I said, feigning a nonchalance I didn't quite feel, "what's this all about? Inquiring minds want to know." I could only imagine that it must be something about her physical condition that for some reason she'd decided not to entrust to her husband/mouthpiece. Or maybe it was something about her estate. Or maybe—

"It's about your daddy," she said. Okay, didn't see that coming. What could there be to say about Lance Rousseau, now thirteen years molderin' in the grave, that warranted a hospital bed pow-wow?

"Dad?" I heard a nervous laugh leak from between my clenched teeth. "What about him?" Clara reached over and placed a hand over one of mine. She looked into my eyes, an odd little smile lifting the corners of her mouth.

"Lance was your daddy," she said, slowly and carefully, "but he wasn't your father."

I let loose a laugh; but Clara wasn't laughing with me.

"Oh, shit," I said (without so much as an "excuse my French"). "You're not kidding."

9.

I took another sip from the glass of cold water Clara had offered me from her handy little swing-away bed tray. I fought the urge to douse my head with it.

"But I look like him," I said. Clara shook her head.

"Oh, you favor him enough to get by," she said, "but that was just luck. Mostly, you look like me." She reached into the pocket of her housecoat, pulled out a piece of what looked like very old paper, and held it out to me. "And him."

I took from her hand what turned out to be an old snapshot, wrinkled and worn to nearly cloth-like softness. Amid a mesh of wrinkles, I could discern the face of a young black man in a soldier's uniform, peaked cap parked at an angle on his head; a faded black-and-white image of a man with my nose, my uneven hairline, and something very like my smile. I said, "Holy shit," followed immediately by "excuse my French." Clara just shrugged one shoulder. "So," I said, looking up from the photograph but not letting it go, "you gonna tell me about this or what?"

"That's why you're sittin' here, baby." She leaned back against the pillows and took a deep breath, then let it out. She took a moment, as if deciding just where to begin, and then began: "Well, you know I come from some poor, backward folks. Daddy and Muh and eleven kids in that raggedy-ass house. Didn't have an indoor toilet in it 'til I was a teenager." I knew the house she was talking about: my maternal grandparents had lived in that house (albeit repaired, improved and with indoor plumbing installed) well into my teen years, usually in the midst of raising one or more grandchildren (my cousin Walter— Theo's only child—spent nearly his entire childhood with Grandma Mary and Grandpa Sherman). I'd visited there with Clara and Lance and my brother David often, usually once a year at minimum, until I left home for college. A squat wooden rectangle with a rambling collection of clapboard and plaster add-ons, perched on low stilts against the inevitable, semi-regular rising of water; sitting on the side of a road that remained unpaved until well into the 1970s.

"And five daughters," Clara continued, looking up at the blank television screen as if Vanna were flipping vowels. "I was number four, and all I ever heard was 'Can't wait 'til you're out of here.'" She looked back at me, a sour little smile on her face. "And God knows, I wanted out. And marrying was what it took to get out." She pointed a forefinger in my direction. "But I didn't want to marry just anybody. I wanted to marry Lance Rousseau." Her smile sweetened and eyelids gently shut as she said, "I'd been in love with him since I was six years old and he was ten." She opened her eyes, and sighed—I mean a big, audible sigh, like in a B romantic comedy.

"You were crazy about him," I said, voicing the obvious. "I don't remember that." In all of my childhood memories, I couldn't recall ever seeing that look on my mother's face. Until her marriage to Daniel Weinberger, I didn't remember ever seeing my mother as a woman in love.

"You were too young," she said, still smiling. "But I *was* crazy about Lance. And he loved me; don't think he didn't. Lance was good to me, at first. For a while. Up until I decided I wanted to go to college and get my degree—in just about anything, just to do it. You and David were both in school, and I was in the house all day long, by myself. But Lance told me no."

"Just no? Just like that?"

"Just like that," she said, nodding. "Never gave me a good reason why. I think he just didn't want me having more education than he had. When you heard us fightin', that's what we were fightin' about, every time. He just didn't want me to grow. Probably scared I wouldn't want to stay with him anymore." She shrugged. "And then I ended up leaving his ass, anyway, and went to school. But when we were kids, seemed like I couldn't want anything in this world like I wanted Lance."

"When I was twelve, he called, trying to court me, told me he loved me, said he'd marry me. But Lance couldn't wait for me." She shook her head and then added, "Loved to screw." I sputtered a laugh. Mother giggled like a naughty schoolgirl, shrugged her shoulders, and said, "He was fine as wine in the summertime, and stickin' it everywhere. So when he was sixteen, seventeen maybe, he got that ho, Annie-Belle, pregnant, and her daddy made him marry her. And she had that little retard of hers and that was the end of it." I got an all-too-clear mental video of my half-brother, Andrew, who my parents told me was my cousin—I found out the true story through sheer blind chance when I was in my mid-thirties, and not from my folks, either. Andrew had been severely impaired, a perpetual infant, pulling himself along the floor in diapers until the day he died, well into adulthood. I pushed the image from my mind, replacing it with Joe's face, just to get the bad taste out of my ... well, mind.

Clara leaned back into the pillows again, her eyes gently shut.

"Mom?" I said, tapping the top of her foot. This was no time for a nap. "What about soldier boy?" I wiggled the old photo.

"Oh," she said, her eyes opened. "Travis. Travis Green. He'd come to St. Charles to bury some relative of his. His mother?" she asked herself, eyes turned toward the ceiling. "His daddy? Anyway, I was walking home from the store in Dogtown—you remember that little store?" she asked me. I nodded. I did, indeed remember. "Cousin Mae-Mae ran it." I remembered Cousin Mae-Mae, too: black, round, and shiny as an old Mammy cookie jar; she was known to give my brother and me free penny candies, just for being whatever kin we allegedly were. "Anyway," Clara said, "he drove up alongside me, in that car of his. Fifty Chevy." She nodded her own agreement. "Only car I'd seen on the road in St. Charles that wasn't an old piece of crap. Or a truck."

"How old were you?" I asked. I needed some context.

"Seventeen," she said. "Almost eighteen. Just graduated high school."

I could see her, a mental image composed of a dimly remembered school photograph of Clara combined with my own all-too-vivid imagination: pretty, dimple-cheeked, chocolate-colored girl, hair hot-combed and pulled back into a rather stiff ponytail; perky boobs barely held in check by bra and white cotton blouse (both hand-me-downs); and long legs shiny with Vaseline leading up to bodacious booty in hand-me-down (of course) skirt, making her way home, shakin' that thang like the girl just naturally does (not meaning anything by it, that's just the way it all moves), her worn-out sneakers (pinky toe peaking out of a little hole in the right one) scattering the bits of seashell that pass for pavement on what passes for the road back from Dogtown (itself little more than a filling station and Mae-Mae's store).

"He rolled the window down," Clara said, "asked me if I wanted a ride. Of course, I said no, thank you, just the same." She smiled with the face of a young girl, and then added, "the first time." She smiled again. "By the third time, I was feelin' that bag of groceries, so I got in. Didn't hurt that he was the best-looking man I'd ever seen in St. Charles, aside from Lance Rousseau." Her smile faded a bit.

"But it was just a ride in a handsome man's big fancy car. For me, anyway. Travis had other ideas. He told me later, he knew he was going to marry me, the first time he saw me. I wasn't even thinking about marriage. Couldn't have Lance, so I was thinking about going back to school, become a nurse." Her eyes closed as she laughed softly to herself. "When I told my daddy that, he said, 'Now who goin' hire a little nigger nurse?'" She made a face, as if she could smell somebody's bedpan. "Travis asked to meet my mother and daddy before he'd even got me all the way home. And Muh and Da, they took one look at that car and that suit and that fedora of his and must have thought Santa Claus came early. Muh sat him down in the front room, filled him full of ice tea and tea-cakes, then invited him to supper."

Clara turned toward the screen divider. I wondered if she'd detected some sound or movement from her roommate, but there had been none. After a moment, she said, "Right after supper, Travis asked Da if he could marry me, and Da said yeah before Travis was through asking." She turned back to me. "Never did ask *me*."

We both turned toward the door at the sound of a theatrical "ahem." As he was wont to do, Daniel had appeared, seemingly out of nowhere, without a sound.

"The Shadow returns," I quipped in my best Eve Arden wisecracking dame voice.

"You should rest," Daniel said, addressing Clara as if I and my quip had never occurred.

"Ten minutes?" Clara said, cap-covered head cocked to one side, eyes widening with flirtation; though lying prone in a hospital bed, her feminine wiles were quite undiminished.

"Ten minutes," Daniel repeated, looking first at his wife, then at me. "I'll be back," he said starting down the hall.

Clara sniffed a little laugh, then said, "Like Arnold." She took in a big breath, blew it out, and said, "Well, I better hurry up." She opened her mouth to speak, then stopped. "Where was I?"

"He never did ask me," I said.

"'Ask me' what?"

"To *marry* you," I prompted.

"And we didn't even get married," she said, suddenly back in the story, hip-deep. "Not in St. Charles, anyhow. Travis slept in the front room on the couch that evening and the next morning I got in that car with him—me and my little cardboard suitcase full of everything I had in the world. And we drove to New York. *New York*," she repeated, as if Travis Green had driven her to Pluto. Though I suppose it may as well have been. "Got married at the justice of the peace, in Harlem." She fell back against the pillows, closed her eyes, and laughed. "Lord have mercy," she said through a chuckle, "you should have seen this poor little country child in New York."

"I can imagine," I said, imagining a lost lamb in a concrete jungle, jumpy and wide-eyed in the face of the speed and noise and the skyscrapers of the big city.

Clara drew her knees up and leaned forward, resting her crossed arms on her knees. "Turned out Travis didn't have a pot to piss in. Car wasn't even his—he'd borrowed it for the trip South. I'd never even thought to ask what he did for a living—don't think Muh and Daddy even cared. Turned out he was a driver, a chauffeur. For this Jew lawyer, who lived up on Park Avenue."

"Sounds like *A Raisin in the Sun*," I said.

Clara smiled, nodded. "I never thought of that," she said. "But it was. Only Travis was fairer-skinned than Sidney Poitier. And of course, I was prettier than Ruby Dee." She laughed through her teeth, *tiss, tiss, tiss*. "Little tiny upstairs apartment, bathroom down the hall."

I made a face at the imagined squalor. "Must have been miserable."

She looked askance. "Child," she said, "I thought I'd died and gone to Glory."

"You're joking."

"Who you kidding? A whole apartment for just me and Travis? I was used to a house *full*. We had to share the bathroom, but at least it was inside. Who you kidding? Didn't even mind the sex."

I squirmed a little.

"And I didn't know a thing," she said, rolling her eyes up toward the acoustic ceiling. "Didn't even know you had to open your legs to do it. Only problem was," she said with a little shrug of her shoulders, "I was still in love with Lance. But," and she shrugged again, "yet and still, it wasn't a bad life. Made Travis's breakfast, packed his lunch to take to work, cooked his dinner—" She laughed a little, reached over and squeezed my hand. "—it took him a year to stop me calling it *supper.* That, and open my legs a couple, three times a week. I'd had it worse."

I was considering asking her to fast-forward to the *me* part of the saga, when she parked her chin into her palm and continued. "About six months in, Travis came home and said the family he drove for lost their governess. Then he explained to me what in the world was a governess. He asked me if I thought I could do it and I said I'd been takin' care of kids my whole life. So I went to work." She just nodded to herself for a moment, while I remembered the picture of that plump, pretty, colored girl and her two little white-boy charges, realizing that (like me) they'd both be middle-aged men now.

"Somewhere in there, I got pregnant, and everybody agreed I'd work until I couldn't. And then—" She stopped short, looking furtively toward the doorway. "Never mind, I thought that was Daniel. Anyway, I was five months pregnant, with you, when I got a letter. From Lance. Had got the address from Muh. That ho, Annie-Belle, had left, just left her baby with her mother and left town with a cousin of hers, talkin' about goin' to San Antonio."

She hugged her knees up close. "He asked me to leave Travis, come back to Louisiana, and move to California with him. *Told* me more than asked me. I wrote back, told him I was about to have Travis's baby. He said he didn't care. He said he'd raise my child as his own, if I'd leave Travis." My mother looked into my face, the fluorescent light glistening in her big, almond-shaped eyes. "And he did. Didn't he?"

And if I hesitated a moment before answering my mother's very-possibly-rhetorical question, it was only because somewhere behind the gentle whir of the air conditioning from the overhead vent, I could hear celestial choirs, heaven's Andrews Sisters singing "Battle Hymn of the Republic," because as it turned out, Lance Rousseau wasn't my father. All the years (and believe me, we're talking a lifetime here) of trying to please my dad into something approximating the obvious love and acceptance he showered on my kid brother (and make no mistake, I tried hard) and, at last, I knew why it had always been a lost cause. Aside from the fact that my brother David was a star little league pitcher and I was a boy soprano until I was nearly fourteen; notwithstanding the fact that while Dad and David tossed a football around the front lawn, I was in my bedroom lip-synching the *Funny Girl* soundtrack album; apart from my brother's presumed heterosexuality (he died too young for anyone to be completely certain) and my own—well, *you* know; the fact of the matter was that every time Lance Rousseau looked at me, until the day he died (okay the day *before* he died, which was the last time he actually did look at me), I might as well have had a tattoo across my forehead saying "Some Other Man's Child."

Finally, I remembered to say to my mother, "Yes. Yes, he did."

She looked at me blankly and said, "Did what?" My face must have fallen visibly as I assumed my mother's mind had experienced yet another glitch. Suddenly, she smiled wide, slapped the back of my hand, and said, "Psych!" I hardly had time to register the surprise when from the doorway came Daniel's voice: "That was actually fifteen minutes." I raised a forefinger in Daniel's direction in the international sign for "just one more quick question and I'll get out of your wife's hospital bed, I promise."

"Mom," I asked, bringing one hand to rest on her housecoat-covered knee, "why are you telling me all this now? After, lo, these many years?"

She covered my hand with hers and smiled an odd little smile (just lips, no teeth, and the barest hint of dimple). "I'm probably gonna die soon, baby. Even if I didn't have this doggone tumor in my head, chances are, I was gonna go first. I didn't want you to hear it from somebody else."

I gathered my mother into a rather awkward sort of half-sitting, half-kneeling hug, kissed both her Seminole cheekbones, and slid out of the bed. Daniel took a step or two into the room.

"Thank you for your patience, Dr Weinberger."

"You have your key to the house," Daniel said, in kind of a semi-question. I nodded that I did have it.

"I'll be back in the morning," I said to Clara, and had one foot in the hall when I heard her say, "Didn't you ever wonder why we never celebrated our wedding anniversary? Lance and me?" I turned back toward her, now reclining on her side, head atop a stack of pillows. It had never occurred to me to wonder about anniversary celebrations or lack thereof. Near as I could tell, Lance was never what I would call the romantic type. I don't recall him ever giving his wife a birthday present, either.

"You were born Christmas Day, 1956," she said. "But Travis wouldn't give me a divorce for quite a while. He was hurt, of course. So I went and lived with Lance, moved to LA with him. But we didn't get married until 1959, when I was pregnant with David. And we both figured sooner or later, you'd do the math. So we just let it go."

"And Travis Green?" I asked.

Clara shrugged. "Dead, I guess. But I don't know. After the divorce, I never looked back."

Well, there was just no response for that except, "Good night, Mother."

"Good night, baby." Out of my peripheral vision, I barely saw Daniel taking his rightful place in the chair next to his wife's bed as I headed down the hall toward the elevators.

I couldn't say for sure if my mother's little surprise had anything to do with the decision that came to me shortly before turning into the gated entryway to the community where resided Dr and Mrs Daniel Weinberger, out of seeming nowhere and in the middle of "Cotton Avenue" from Joni's *Don Juan's Reckless Daughter* album, but by the time Domingo, the portly Latino security guard (who had recently learned to recognize me by sight) opened the tastefully ornate iron gate for me, I knew that as soon as possible after returning home, I was going to ask Joe Callahan—former porn performer, ex-call boy, current love of my life—to move in with me.

10.

I had brand new taper candles and half a dozen sterling roses (just sort of loitering in a crystal vase) on the dining room table. I had boneless, skinless chicken breasts sautéed with garlic, keeping warm on the stove. I had Mathis on the stereo—so old-school it's practically Jurassic, I know, but when it comes to romance, nobody can croon it like Johnny. And, I had a freshly stamped house key in my pocket—for Joe. I was washing a colander full of allegedly prewashed spinach under the kitchen faucet (damned if I'm ever gonna lose a filling in a salad) when I heard the front door open and Joe call out "Hey, Daddy." I wiped my hands dry on a dishtowel and met Joe a few steps into the foyer.

As usual, we tasted one another's tongue and felt each other up, by way of hello. We stood for a moment, arms around each other, my hands tucked into the back pockets of Joe's double-stuffed Levi's, until he said, "I have news."

I said, "So do I," and kissed him on the rounded tip of his nose.

"What is it?" he asked.

"You first."

"Okay," he said, stepping back a bit, just enough to break the embrace. "I've been asked to go on tour with *Naked Truth*."

My old friend the imp was back, laughing like Woody Woodpecker as he executed a flying drop-kick to my guts. "I'm sorry," I said. "You what?"

"They're going to mount the play in San Francisco this fall. Then maybe Philadelphia. And, we hope, New York. Off-Broadway." Joe smiled with every tooth in his head. He was bouncing up and down on the balls of his sneakered feet like a little kid. His excitement was in the air like too much cheap aftershave.

I asked the inevitable stupid question: "Are you going?" Naturally, he looked at me as if I'd taken leave of every sense I'd ever claimed to have. A nervous, ragged little laugh escaped his lips.

"Of course I'm going," he said.

"Oh," was the best I could do under the circumstances. I removed myself from our semi-embrace and walked toward the living room. "Let's all sit down, shall we?"

"Oh, fuck," I heard from behind me. "What is it?" I tipped myself backward to land in my favorite armchair, my heart rapping the staccato drum solo from the Fight or Flight Boogie. As so often happens when my emotions are threatening to burst the levees like Katrina's worst night, I went totally Bette Davis, my voice a bit too loud, a tad high-pitched, and my words bitten off like taffy when I looked up at Joe (standing a safe distance from my chair) and said,

"You didn't ask me what my news is."

Joe backed into the twin armchair across the coffee table from me and sat down. I watched his lips attempt a smile, without much success. He said, "What's your news, Johnnie?"

I reached into the right front pocket of my jeans (a maneuver which required a certain amount of squirming in my chair), retrieved the house key I'd had made that afternoon, and tossed it onto the table. It bounced once (*ting!*) and lay there, shiny as an engagement ring and (for me) nearly as significant.

"Key to my house," I said, still Bette Davis, loud, hip-deep in Auntie territory, and not giving a damn. "I was going to ask you to come live with me. That's my news."

I watched Joe's gaze move from the key on the table between us, up to my face, then back down to the table. It was as much to the key as to me that he said, "Wow."

"Wow, indeed," I said. I'm sure Joe had not walked in expecting a full-blown diva scene, but he was headed straight for one: I could feel it building up inside me. "No fool like and old fool, huh?"

"What do you mean by that?" Joe gripped the chair arms as if to get up, as if to come toward me, then dropped back down into the chair. I suspect I was a bit frightening.

"What I *mean* by that is," in full-blown Bette, leaning forward from the waist, "when you told me you loved me, I was foolish enough to believe you might actually have *meant* it."

Joe leaned in, his voice nearly as loud as mine (though not nearly as strident): "I do love you, Johnnie. You know that."

"Only you'd rather traipse across the country playing soft porn—"

"It is *not* porn!" Joe shouted, a curl I'd never seen before on his lips.

"Well, you of all people would know," I tossed off from the corner of my mouth.

Joe fairly leapt from the chair, pointed a blunt, meaningful index finger in my direction, and shouted, "I'm not ashamed of anything I've done," he slashed the air with that finger. "Anything. I'm not ashamed of anything I'm *going* to do ..." He opened his mouth to speak, closed it, looked around the room as if following the flight of a mosquito, and then added, "and please just fucking *forgive* me for not being forty-eight years old."

"What?" I shrieked. It was an *All About Eve* noise if I'd ever made one. I sat up yardstick-straight.

"You don't look your age, Johnnie," he said, "not nearly. But you're pushing fifty. I'm thirty-one. You've had your career, you're practically retired. But I'm ..." he watched the invisible mosquito for a moment, searching for words. "I'm still trying to find my way, what I am, what I'm gonna be." He crossed his big arms across his chest, making his pecs bulge, the hottest angry young man in town. "I'm not stupid, Johnnie" he said.

"I—"

"I know *Naked Truth* isn't *Long Day's Journey Into* fuckin' *Night*. But it's acting. It's a start. I hope it is, anyway." And suddenly, Joe's protuberant lower lip was quivering, fat tears fell from the corners of his eyes, and he pushed them back with the heels of his hands. "I thought you'd be happy for me," he said through a bubble of mucus.

I was up out of my chair, rounding the coffee table, and almost to Joe before I realized I was crying, too. I reached for Joe, repeating "I'm sorry, I'm sorry, I'm sorry." Joe pushed me away, but his heart wasn't in it, and I gathered his broad shoulders in my arms and called him Baby and we cried a while, just holding each other and crying like children, loudly and without shame.

And it was during that unlikely spectacle that it occurred to me that I'd played something very like this scene before. It came to mind like an old movie I hadn't seen since high school: my lover, my life partner Keith Keller telling me he needed a husband, someone who'd be home for dinner at the same time every evening and next to him in bed every night; not some crazy thing that sings in bars and clubs and cabarets until morning. And me, telling Keith that singing was everything to me, telling him goodbye.

And I knew then and there, with my buffed, beautiful man-child Joe sniffing snot in my arms, what I needed to do. I took my hands off of Joe and took a step back away from him.

I said, "I think you should go," realizing by the time the words had left my mouth, just how unclear I'd been. "I think you should go on tour," I said slowly and carefully. "And, I think you should go away, now."

"Are we breaking up?" he asked, looking up at me, crossing his arms over his deep chest again.

"Yes, Baby-boy. We are breaking up."

"You don't really want that," he said, shaking his head no.

"No," I agreed, and took a step closer to Joe, still not touching him. "No. What I want is for you to be home for dinner every night at seven and lying in bed next to me at ten. Every night. That's what I want." I couldn't quite stifle a little sniff of a laugh: this was as big a helping of what-goes-around-comes-around as I could imagine, and it was about as appetizing as a platter of deep-fried hell. I could hear my old pal the imp, sitting on my left shoulder, having the laugh of his miniature cherry-red life.

Joe just looked at me for a long moment. I watched the left side of his lips lift into something that wasn't quite a smile. "I'd better go now," he said.

I nodded and extended my right hand. Joe took it in his left. We walked slowly to my front door, hand in hand. We kissed on the lips as I pulled the door open.

"I do love you, Daddy," he said.

"I know." I allowed myself a long last look at that amazing porno-butt walking away, then pushed the door closed.

And proceeded to drink an entire bottle of Pino Grigio as I watched *Maurice* in its entirety, while my dinner blackened on the stove.

The resulting depression was immediate and so deep it went halfway to China. I couldn't even drag my ass out of bed the next morning. Through the throbbing wine-head, I remembered I was scheduled to serve communion that morning. I belly-crawled to the bedside phone and pressed the church phone number without even opening my eyes. When I told Pastor Tom I was sick, it wasn't a lie: my head was threatening to split like an overripe Crenshaw melon on the sidewalk in the summertime, and whatever it was I had left in my stomach from the day before (I'd eaten no dinner) was threatening a comeback. I slept through Sunday in its entirety (I seem to recall making my way to the toilet for some explosive diarrhea at least once), then called in sick to work at some point early Monday morning, leaving a message on Harold's voice mail that must have sounded like a visit from beyond the grave. I may well have slept through Monday as well, if Amos and Andy hadn't decided enough was enough, rattling the bedroom door so loud I thought it might be a thunderstorm, singing the feline version of some Wagnerian duet at their full vocal capacity (which was considerable).

I pushed myself up and out of bed. When my feet touched the

carpet, I looked down and realized I was still wearing one Sperry Top-Sider. In fact, other than one shoe, I was fully dressed in jeans and polo shirt. The inside of my mouth felt as if it was made entirely of ground glass and my left eye was crusted shut because I'd slept for the better part of two days with my contact lenses in. I opened the bedroom door and my cats burst in (scolding in loud voices), followed immediately by enough sunlight to knock me back onto the bed.

"Okay," I said in response to their yowling, "I'll feed you in a minute." The yowling continued unabated as I stumbled to the bathroom, both cats head-butting my ankles and swatting at my shins with their tails. The thing looking back at me from the bathroom mirror was more hideous than I'd feared. I detected an odor not unlike two-days-dead road kill and surmised quickly that it was my breath. I washed my hands with antibacterial soap and water as hot as I could stand, then reached through the gobs of grey-green gunk in and around my eyes and pulled out my contacts. From the tearing sound it made, I wouldn't have been surprised to find I'd peeled off my corneas. I flicked the gack-encrusted lenses from my fingers and into the waste-basket, fished my glasses out of the vanity drawer, and pushed them onto my face.

The *katzenjammer* grew more insistent by several decibel levels, reminding me to prioritize. I started toward the computer/cat room with a limp, then kicked off my remaining shoe and shuffled the rest of the way, my legs as heavy as a heroin habit. I refilled the empty cat bowls (Amos and Andy finally stopped shouting at me as they threw themselves face-first into the food, crunching kibble with an amazing amount of motion and sound), and scooped out the litter box, wondering aloud if they might have had house guests—two cats couldn't possibly create that much waste in a paltry two days. I was bundling up a truly astounding amount of kitty poop and baseball-sized litter clumps into some newspaper when the phone rang, the sound hitting my tender head like a sprinter's shoe, cleats first. I cried out in pain, managed to lift myself from full squat in time to pick up on the third excruciating ring, and croaked Hello.

"Johnnie." I recognized Sully's voice through the ringing in my ears and what seemed to be a head cold on Sully's end.

"Sullivan? Are you all right?"

"I called your office," he said, still sounding as if he'd been blowing his nose for hours at a time, "and they said you were out sick."

"No, I'm okay," I fibbed. "Just didn't feel like going into work. Taking a little mental health day."

"Oh, good," he said. Between the glob of silly putty I was currently using for a brain and whatever was going on with Daniel Sullivan, there was a maybe thirty-second stretch of silence (during which I began to comprehend the severity of my own bodily odor).

Finally, I said, "So what's up, Sully?" At which I could have sworn I heard a sob. A butch, baritone sob, but a sob. "Sully?" Another sob, after which he said,

"I need to talk to you, Johnnie. I need to see you. Please."

Oh, Sweet Mary, what could it be now? "What is it, Sully? What's wrong, buddy?"

"I just," he stammered, "I need to talk to you, Johnnie. May I come over?"

To say I wasn't exactly ready to play the hostess was an understatement of historic proportions, but a hulking straight guy was weeping into a telephone—what else could I say except, "Of course, Sully. Come on over."

I'd managed a shower, a much-needed tooth brushing, and a hemp-protein smoothie (all of which helped me feel a bit more like a higher primate) by the time Sully came a-knocking at my door.

One look at my buddy's face told me this was going to be no picnic. The wardrobe was business casual (tasseled Italian loafers, slacks, dress shirt open at the neck), but the face was funereal. Sully has one of those pale but florid Caucasian faces that reacts to crying by going all red and blotchy. Judging from the mottled mess beneath Sullivan's expensive, short haircut, he had been weeping for awhile. He blinked rapidly a few times, sniffed wetly and said, "May I come in?"

Sully followed me into the living room. I gestured for him to sit in an armchair and pulled its twin over from across the coffee table and sat. My living room had apparently become Drama Central. I looked at Sully, his big body crumpled in the chair like a piece of waste paper, and silently wished he'd open up the proceedings. He stared at the hairy backs of his own hands for what struck me as an uncomfortable interim.

"May I get you something to drink?" I asked. He started, as if awakened from sleep. "No," he said, his eyes Bambi big. "I have to go back to work."

"I meant a glass of water."

"Oh," he said, and a mirthless little laugh puffed between his lips. And suddenly he blurted, "I've been cheating on Maggie." He took an audible breath in and out, then added, "My wife."

I fell back into my chair. "Aw, shit." Before I could decide whether or not to ask questions, interview him like Oprah, he looked back down at his hands and said, "He works at the firm." I popped up like a jack-in-the-box. *He?*

Sullivan was making an intense visual study of the fabric covering his knees, seemingly avoiding my eyes at all costs.

"I'm bisexual," he said, "to answer the unspoken question. But that's never really mattered, not since I've been married." He suddenly looked up at me (startling me just a bit) and said, "I love my wife." Several smart-ass retorts crossed my mind (none of which I was tasteless enough to verbalize) by the time Sully said, "I never meant for it to happen." I was thinking, Hell, who does? when he turned his head slightly, looking toward the window where a smattering of small birds was flying by. He spoke as if I was standing off to the side rather than sitting across from him.

"I was working late one night, pulling some documents together for a depo prep." He turned away from the window and looked down at his own hands. "I'd been pulling a lot of late nights for this case." It occurred to me that Sully was going to monologue for a bit, like Anne Baxter in *All About Eve*, so I settled back in my chair.

"He came to my office to deliver this huge copy job. My door was open and he knocked at the doorjamb to get my attention. I'd noticed him before." Sully looked up at me, an odd little smile on his lips. "He's a good-looking guy," Sully shrugged his big shoulders, "even though he's not really my type."

"Latino?" I said.

Sully looked askance and said, "How'd you know he was Latino?"

"He's making photocopies in a Century City law firm. Stands to reason."

Sully said, "Hector. He's big, almost as big as I am. Definitely not my type. I tend to like smaller guys, but muscular. Like you."

"And Crockett Miller," I said. The color fell from Sully's face at the mention of our departed mutual friend, then he blushed crimson all the way to his earlobes.

"Yeah," he said, nodding. "So anyway, Hector puts the boxes of copies down on the floor and it's like he doesn't want to leave. Starts making stupid small talk, like 'Working late tonight, huh?' And he's wearing this little short-sleeve polo shirt all the guys in the copy room have to wear, and he's got these big arms, big chest. And I made some comment. You know, just a regular guy kind of comment, like 'The guns are looking good,' or something. And then he says, 'How about this?' And he pulls his shirt up and flexes his abs at me."

"Wow." The mental picture was a nice one.

"Yeah. That's just what *I* said. And I must have been pretty damn obvious because Hector shuts the door behind him and locks it. And ..." Sully once again found it uncomfortable to look me in the face, and looked down to study the backs of his hands again. "One thing led to another."

"Exactly what things were they?" I asked. Sully snorted a little laugh.

"Not much, really. He sucked me, sucked me off. Jacked off. That's all he wanted." He shrugged again. "It's all he ever wants."

I let that hang in the air a moment, and then said, "So I take it you've been working more late nights than usual?" Sully nodded.

"I'm trying to figure out how to tell Maggie." He was still looking at his hands, clenching and straightening his fingers in his lap.

"How to tell Maggie *what*?" I asked.

"About this. I have to tell her."

"May one venture to ask why? Are you in love with this Hector person? Are you planning to leave your wife for him?"

Sully looked at me as if I'd suddenly begun speaking Pig Latin. "No," he said. "Of course not." He sort of shrugged. "I just feel so fucking guilty," he said.

I'm still not sure what possessed me. Heaven knows, I was still reeling from the oh-so-recent breakup with my Joe and my head was decidedly less than clear of my good friend, Mr Hangover. But I could swear I actually heard something snap (and it wasn't my left kneecap this time) as I pushed myself up from the chair and stood in front of Sully.

"Look at me," I said.

Sully tilted his movie star-handsome face up to me, his expression of blank expectation.

I said, "Have you ever seen the movie *Moonstruck*?"

Sully nodded, a raised eyebrow indicating his puzzlement at the non sequitur. "Cher, right?"

"Right," I said. "Remember this?" After which I smacked my buddy across the face just as hard as I could swing, and shouted, "Snap out of it!"

Sully started, pushed against the arms of the chair as if to get up (and very likely deck me), and then didn't. He looked at me, and then away from me, shook his head as if to clear it, then lifted one big hand to his face, fingertips gingerly touching the spot where I'd hit him, where a livid handprint was already appearing. Finally, he looked back at me, his face agape with pain and confusion and said, "What the *fuck*, Johnnie?" He touched his cheek again and added, "You fuckin' *hit* me!"

"Yeah," I said. "I'm a hitter now. Did I hurt you?"

"Damn *right* you hurt me," he shouted.

"Good," I said, sitting back in my chair. "Then I've got your undivided attention." I crossed my legs at the knees, crossed my arms tight across my chest, and said, "So you feel guilty, do you? Well, you know something, buddy? Nut up! *Live* with it. Don't you dare try to lighten your guilty conscience by running home and spilling this tawdry little tale to Maggie. You just *suffer*, bitch. And in silence, if you please."

Sully made a sour face. "Jesus, Johnnie."

"Well, what did you want from me, Sully? Sympathy? I mean, what were you thinking?" I uncrossed and recrossed my legs in rapid succession. "I'm a guy. I realize we all think with our dick sometimes. And from what I understand, your dick's bigger than some guys' brains." Sully blushed to match the mark I'd put on his cheek. "But Daniel, you're an attorney. I believe you've heard of sexual harassment?"

"I know," he said to his lap.

"This big cha-cha could turn around and sue you *and* your firm, you know that don't you?"

"I know," he repeated.

"Well?" I shouted. Bette Davis was back. "What have you got to say for yourself?"

He looked at me and shouted back, "I'm fifty-one years old, Johnnie! And I don't look thirty-five, like you. I've got luggage under my eyes and I've got my father's belly, and Hector," suddenly he avoided my eyes again, "Hector made me feel ..." Sully rolled his eyes. "He makes me feel hot, okay? He calls me '*papi.*' Keeps telling me how much he loves my ... my cock." He blushed some more. "Maggie, well she doesn't like to suck me. And more and more, when we make love, she says it hurts." He shot up a warning forefinger as if to cut me off. "I'm not saying this is Maggie's fault, not one bit. It's just that ..." He closed his eyes, tilted his head back. "You must have some idea what I'm talking about," he said. He lifted his head and looked me in the face. "I mean, Joe's so much younger than you."

The tears were burning my eyes before Sully had finished the sentence.

"We broke up," I said, hardly managing a good whisper.

"Oh, fuck, Johnnie." Sully reached out a hand, but he was too far away to touch me; leaned forward as if he might leave the chair, then didn't. "I'm sorry, man."

The tears fell and I just let them.

"This isn't about me," I said, saltwater bubbling at the back of my throat. "This is about you. You have a wife, Sully. Who loves you, and will stay with you until the day you die. Someone to grow old with." I looked at Sullivan through a warped window of tears. "That should make you feel pretty hot, *papi*." Next I knew, Sully was kneeling in front of me, one arm rather clumsily around my shoulders, a big, soft paw stroking the side of my head as I sobbed an undignified volume of wetness and noise. "Don't, don't fuck it up, Sully," I said into his chest, gargling my own tears and snot. "Just don't."

"I won't," he whispered into my ear, his head so close to mine I could feel his beard stubble against the side of my face. He held me and rocked me and let me cry until I'd had enough.

Finally, I pushed him gently away. "You should go," I said. "Go back to work. Or better yet, go home and bang the daylights out of your wife." I sniffed, then added, "Gently."

"You gonna be all right?" he asked, then grunted as he rose slowly to his feet (his father's belly undoubtedly tough on his fifty-one-year-old knees).

I looked up at my friend, sniffed back another noseful of mucus and said, "Not today, no. But thanks for asking."

11.

For the next several weeks, okay maybe a couple of months—well into October, actually—I pretty much went through the motions of existence. I mean, it's not as if I went all Howard Hughes, filthy and naked, toenails clicking against the floor. I showered and brushed my teeth on a regular basis. Ate my usual five-to-six small high-protein meals per day, without actually tasting anything. Even went to the gym my wonted three days a week, my Fast and Loud playlist (Hendrix, Led Zep, and "Since U Been Gone" by Kelly Clarkson) blasting through my head, speaking to no one, pretty much looking at no one. I fed my cats and paid my bills and did my laundry.

I even went to work, answering Harold's phone, typing his letters, and finding the files he swore had fallen though the space-time continuum, but were, in point of fact, on his desk being used as a coaster for a Starbuck's tall non-fat latte. I ate my organic cashew butter-on-organic-whole-grain lunches alone at my desk, reading the Bible (King James version, notwithstanding its countless errors in transla-tion; just because I like the language). The office soon became nearly as lonely as my home, as my straight neighbor-slash-buddy, Vince (he of the spiky coiffure and impressive biceps), was summarily shit-canned—his term—from the law firm of Potenza and Dennehy for accidentally emailing a particularly lurid example of photographic pornography entitled "goatse" (Google it yourself—I refuse even to attempt a description) to the entire firm.

Funny: Vince (his obvious visual value aside) had always been as much a distraction and low-grade annoyance as he'd been a friend. And then suddenly, Vince was gone. And then I found I missed him, more than I'd ever have guessed.

I went to church, doing my deacon duty—intoning scripture read-ings I didn't remember two seconds after I'd spoken them, lip-synch-ing hymns that seemed as meaningful as "Ring Around the Rosy" (or maybe less: "ashes, ashes, we all fall down" actually held a certain amount of meaning for me), and greeting members of the flock I helped to tend with hugs and smiles I'm sure held all the warmth of a Corian countertop. When people asked what was wrong (and they did ask), I'd say "I'm fine." And either I was supremely convincing or sufficiently frightening to behold that they feared that delving further might be like slamming a landmine with an Adirondack little league baseball bat with all one's upper body strength.

And, of course, I visited Clara, if not every weekend then at least every other. Her tumor had stopped shrinking, but wasn't growing, either; she counted each successive day of life and relative lucidity a miracle. Clara surmised my problem within a nanosecond of seeing

195

my face. Aside from somehow getting her to believe I was heterosexual for the first seventeen years of my life, putting one over on my mother had never been an option. She could read my face like a back issue of *Ebony*. Clara had kissed me softly on the cheek and said, "Don't give up. There's someone for you."

But mostly, I moped—slouching in front of the television, aimlessly changing channels until my thumb cramped, or simply lying face-down on my bed, smelling Joe's peculiar vanilla-coconut scent in the pillow where his head once lay (I didn't wash that pillow case for weeks, until long after the scent was no longer discernible), listening to later Billie Holiday recordings (including the nearly unlistenable *Lady in Satin*—recorded, it had always seemed to me, mere minutes before her death), the sound of her ravaged voice an aural metaphor for my shredded heart.

It was a Friday evening and I was watching the Judy Garland *A Star Is Born* on DVD (actually, replaying the "Man That Got Away" number over and over, until I'd literally lost count), when there was a *knock knock knock* at the front door. It was with some reluctance that I dropped the universal remote onto the sofa and pulled myself up to a standing position. The second knuckle-triplet against the door was a bit louder and followed immediately by the ringing of the doorbell. "All right, already!" I shouted as I reached for the doorknob.

It actually took me a moment to recognize Dre—both because it had been two or three weeks since I'd seen him (and the past few weeks had, of course, felt like dog years), and because his familiar head full of dreadlocks had been shorn high-and-tight on the sides and back, leaving only a wild Medusa pompadour of dreads falling forward across his forehead. It was a very different look for Dre, and (even through my present near-stupor) it was smokin' hot.

"May I come in?" he asked.

I said, "Of course," and stepped aside, taking in the rest of the sight for sore eyes that was Dre as he walked in: bright orange T-shirt snug enough for me to count his abs, and a pair of stretch jeans.

I pushed the door shut behind me and said, "You look great."

"You look like shit," he said flatly, then started away from me. "Let's all sit down, shall we?" he said in a tone of voice that may well have been a pointed imitation of me. At a loss for what else to do, I followed Dre's epic ass across the house into my family room. He plopped down on the sofa across from the television, where Judy was freeze-framed (mouth wide open, arms outstretched, caught in the middle of the "gone" in "Where's he gone to?"). Dre looked up at me, rolled his eyes, and said, "Judy Garland? Could you be watching anything more tired-old-homo than this?" He picked up the remote from the cushion beside him and clicked the DVD player off. The screen turned bright blue and I lowered myself onto the opposite end of the couch from Dre.

"As it happens," I said, "I am a tired old homo."

"Got that right," he said, twiddling the remote between his fingers.

I felt adrenaline rocket through me. I was just a shout away from snatching the remote from Dre and going upside his head with it. "What are you doing here, Dre? Just thought you'd pop over and insult me for a while?"

He cocked his head to one side. "If that's what it takes."

"If that's what it takes to *what*?"

"To snap your tired old homo butt out of this dreary-ass, Judy Garland-watching pity party."

"Excuse me please," I was up again, arms crossed, head bobbing, "but in case you hadn't noticed, there's some *shit* going on in my life right now. My mother—"

Dre sprung from the sofa, pointing the flying forefinger of accusation in my direction. "Don't you *dare* pull your mama into this."

"What?"

"You and I both know this ain't about your mama. It's about Porno Boy, and that's all it's about, so how about let's cut the *bull*shit, okay?"

I took a big step forward to Dre, made a suitably Garland-esque arm gesture, and shouted, "How *dare* you?"

Dre shifted his weight to one foot, placed fist to hip, and said, "Tell me I'm lyin'."

And I would have, too. If the sumbitch hadn't been so damn right. And then it occurred to me that I hadn't even told Dre about the breakup.

"How the hell did *you* know?" I said.

"Boy, how big a town do you think this is? The WeHo grapevine went buzzin' when you hooked up with Porno Boy, and it was up and down Santa Monica Boulevard five minutes after he walked out your door."

"Fuck." I did a half-turn on my heels and crumpled back into the sofa.

"And by the way: exactly when were you planning to call me, anyway? Make me hear about it on the streets." Dre stood glaring down at me, making me feel like a ten-year-old called to the principal's office. I raised my hands in a silent-film gesture of supplication.

"Please, Dre," I whined, "I don't want to fight. I *can't* fight, I don't have the fuckin' strength, okay?" I looked up at my friend, his sinewy arms wrapped tight around his front, jaws clenched tight. "I don't know why I didn't call you, I really don't." Which I realized was a major league lie as I was telling it. Somewhere underneath my thick, downy blanket of self-pity, I knew I had done Dre wrong. I had pulled the typical nelly-boy trick of becoming so caught up in the hip-swinging, shoulder-shimmying Fosse-esque production number entitled "Being in Love," that I had neglected my best friend. How could I come running back to Dre once the dance was over and I was left the emotional equivalent of a chorus girl with two broken legs?

I lowered my head into my hands and said, "I'm a beaten man, Dre. I've been a Southern fried prick to you and I admit it. But if it makes you feel any better, I'm pretty fucking miserable, okay?"

"Niggah, *please!*" Dre did a knee-drop in front of me and grabbed both my wrists, leaving me no choice but to look him in the face. "You dated a cute boy for a while and then it ended. Get a *grip*, boy!"

"Dre," I said, "I loved him. I said so, right out loud." Following a joyless little laugh, I added, "I hadn't said that to anybody since Keith. I'd waited almost fifteen years after he died before I let myself go, really allowed myself to love somebody. I was ready to give him the key to my house. I was thinking of marrying him, Dre. What the hell was I thinking?"

Dre let go of my wrists. He shook his head, his eyes rolling up toward the ceiling. "Wasn't about what you were thinking," he said, pushing himself to his feet. "It's about what you were thinking *with*."

I stood to face him. "I beg your pardon?" I said with as much indignation as I could muster under the circumstances.

"Johnnie Ray Rousseau, you are without doubt the dumbest *smart* niggah I have ever met." I was stammering something incoherent when Dre continued. "Has it honestly never occurred to you that *I* love you," he poked himself in the chest with an emphatic forefinger, "and would marry your almost-forty-nine-year-old black ass right today?" He shifted his weight from one foot to the other, cocked his head to one side, and dispelled any hope I may have had that he'd asked a rhetorical question by adding, "Well, *has* it?"

Dre made a wide-eyed, purse-lipped face that all but screamed "I'm waiting," but I was quite speechless. Of course, I'd taken it for granted that Dre loved me (in a way) and took it equally for granted that he knew I loved him (in my fashion). "But I assumed you liked things the way they were. Friends. Fuck buds. You've never said otherwise."

Dre parked his fists onto his hips and said, "Well, what was I *supposed* to say, niggah? Mister—" and here Dre executed a dead-on impersonation of me at my hincty best, saying, "I like the rhythm of friendship—here I am, there I go."

And he was right, of course. Dammit-all-to-hell, how I do hate admitting I'm wrong. I felt the tears smarting behind my eyes. I'd managed to fuck up my life so perfectly it was practically an art form, and now I wanted nothing so much as to sit on the floor and cry like a little girl. I blinked the tears back, reached over, and touched the side of Dre's neck with my fingertips.

"I'm so sorry, Dre," I said, and turned away. "Forgive me."

"Forgive my black *ass*," Dre said, grabbing me by the wrist and forcing me to face him. "What part of I love you did you not understand?"

I said, "You're joking, right? After what I've put you through?"

"Yeah," Dre nodded, letting go of my wrist. "After watching you chase the Porno Boy for half a year. Kinda makes me look like a punk, don't it?" And he took my face into his hands and pulled my mouth into his, kissing me hard. He bit my lower lip on the way out, so hard I wasn't sure he was planning to give it back to me. He kept his fingers wrapped around my head, held my forehead against his and whispered, "You love me, Johnnie?"

I nodded, rolling our foreheads together like ball bearings.

"Tell me."

I tasted salt (tears, maybe blood, maybe both) as I said, "I love you, Andre." And we held each other close, an embrace so long and so fierce it was like isometrics, my biceps threatening to cramp after a while. When we finally let go, and we'd finished kissing (lips and tongues, cheeks, eyelids, Dre licking my tears up, and me just this side of hyperventilation), Dre took me by the shoulders, looked into my eyes and simply said, "Good."

And I said, "So, you'll marry me?"

Dre leaned his head away from mine and smiled, shook his head, and said, "No."

"What?" I took a step back. "What are you playing at, anyway?"

"Shorty," he said, "you don't need no husband right now. What you need is a friend. That's what I'm trying to be here. And I sure as shit don't need no husband in the kind of shape you're in right now. 'Cause you're some kind of fucked-up mess at the moment."

"I've *always* been a fucked-up mess," I said, crossing my arms in front of me. I needed somebody's arms around me, if only my own.

"More than usual, Shorty." Dre turned and fell back into the sofa. I didn't follow him; I just stood there, arms crossed, jaws clenched. "I know what you've been through this year, baby. Your mom's sick—"

I took a deep breath and then used it all to correct him: "Dying. My mother is dying. And I've buried three friends this year and we've still got the holidays to get through. And I'm going through a case of the middle-age crazies the likes of which the world has seldom seen."

"My point exactly," Dre said. "Plus, you've just finished making a big fool of yourself over some little ho-ho-ho, young enough to be your child. Emotionally, you're all over the fucking map. Frankly, I deserve better."

I crumpled back into the couch. The man was right. I wouldn't wish me on my worst enemy, let alone my best friend. Still, I couldn't just let it drop. Not if Dre even thought he might love me. Head back, eyes closed, I spoke to the ceiling: "So Dre?"

"So?" he said.

"Do you suppose we might ... date?"

I heard a sputtering little laugh. "Date?"

"Date," I repeated. I lifted my head and turned to look at Dre: he was back to arms-crossed position. "As in, Would you like to have dinner with me? Sometime?"

Dre looked over at me, his facial expression changing second by second, like a flip-book, the last page of which was a decided scowl.

Finally, Dre slid off the sofa, kneeling between my thighs again. Then he smiled, a symphony of teeth and gums, and said, "I'm very fond of dinner."

I felt my face split into a smile. I leaned forward into Dre and we kissed again. I nuzzled his sweet-smelling neck and stroked his broad back.

"But as friends," Dre said, tugging gently at my earlobe with his fingers.

"Friends," I agreed. After a moment, I said, "So, friend: will you come with me to the desert this weekend, to see Clara?"

He let go of my ear and kissed it. "Uh-huh."

I said, "Thanks," and kissed him lightly on the lips. "Oh, and Dre?"

"*Hmm?*"

"Don't ever call me the N-word. You *know* how I hate that."

12.

Clara died on the first of July. At home, in her own bed, with her husband beside her. Which was how she wanted it. She'd had about six really good months—feeling pretty good, her mind fairly close to what it had always been. Daniel took her on an extended cruise through the Caribbean (I got some truly breathtaking postcards and snaps, several weeks after they'd returned). She seemed to be doing pretty well into May, the anniversary of her diagnosis, and then she just seemed to come undone. First the speech slurred, then she began dropping things, like her fork at the dinner table.

The last time I saw her, the third weekend in June, she was having a hard time speaking, so I played DJ on the sleek and expensive stereo system Daniel had bought for her, free-associating my way through Clara's extensive CD collection (most of them formerly mine, handed down over the past couple of years as I slowly went all-digital), and we sat together on Clara's pillow-soft sofa and listened to the music we both loved: some Ray, a bit of Sam Cooke, but mostly old gospel from the 50s and 60s—Mahalia, the Swan Silvertones, and the Five Blind Boys of Mississippi. I closed my eyes and swayed to the music Clara had played during my early childhood, when she'd stack four or five LPs teetering above a tone arm weighted down with a penny to guard against the records' skipping.

At one point, I barely caught the familiar, comforting sound of my mother singing, so softly, lips barely parted, her voice along the top of the heartache tenor of Archie Brownlee of the Five Blind Boys: "If you make it in Glory before I do / Save a seat for me." I squeezed my mother's hand, leaned over and kissed the scarf tied snug around her head, as Daniel appeared (soundlessly and surprisingly as usual) to tell me it was time Clara went to bed.

Back at home, Dre and I were sitting in our bed watching *Yankee Doodle Dandy* (the opening feature of our Fourth of July weekend DVD film festival, which we had planned to include *Independence Day* and *The Music Man*, as well) when the bedside telephone chirped. Dre had started moving his things over to my house in late October. I cleaned out half my dresser drawers for his socks and underwear the week before Thanksgiving. By my forty-ninth birthday, he was visiting his apartment just to pick up mail. Come the New Year, he gave up his place altogether. He was teaching science, PE, and a couple of dance classes at a private middle school in Cheviot Hills, and didn't miss dancing for a living, or so he claimed. We cooked dinner together most evenings, slept entangled every night. I could tell you I wasn't loving it, but you'd know I was lyin'.

Jimmy Cagney was in the middle of the tap break in the "Give My

Regards to Broadway" number when the sound of the phone gave me a start. My nasty little red imp executed a flying drop-kick to my midsection, and I knew it was The Call. Dre paused the DVD (James Cagney frozen in mid-air, tap-shoes hovering just above the stage floor). He must have seen the premonition in my eyes, because he picked up the receiver and handed it right to me. I said, "Daniel."

I heard him say, "She's left us, John."

I said, "I'm so sorry, Daniel." True, I had lost my mother, my friend, my hero. But I had had Clara for nearly fifty years—Daniel for less than twenty. "Thanks for letting me know."

"I'll talk to you tomorrow, the next day," he said. "About the service and … I've got a lot of phone calls to make."

"I'll come over in the morning and help with that," I said.

"I couldn't ask you to do that."

"Daniel," I said, "I'm a secretary. It's what I do."

After a moment, he said, "Thank you, John. Johnnie. I'd appreciate that."

When I handed Dre the telephone, he just said, "I'm so sorry, baby." I just nodded. There was nothing to say. "You all right?" he asked.

I nodded again, then said, "Yeah. I'm all right." And I actually was. Because my mother and I had both lived long enough to become friends again after those ugly years immediately following my coming out. Because after years of relative misery with the man I'd believed was my father, Clara had spent her final couple of decades as the wife of a man who worshipped her black ass—and she died a rich, very happy lady. And because I knew in my heart that, having made it to Glory first, she was saving a seat for me.

Dre returned the phone to its cradle. Then he took my right hand in both of his and kissed the back of it, and then the palm, then nestled it against his long-muscled, sweatpants-covered thigh.

"Dre?" I said.

"Yes, Shorty."

"Marry me?"

He inclined his head (hair clipped short, the slightest hint of grey at the temples—the head of a schoolteacher) toward me, tilted my face up to his with his fingertips, and kissed my lips.

He said, "Yes, Shorty." Then he released my hand and retrieved the remote control. Suddenly, there was music, and Cagney's tap shoes touched lightly down onto the stage, and his squat but nimble Irish legs carried him along, an embodiment of staccato grace in glorious black-and-white.

Acknowledgments

The author would like to thank Don Weise, Michael Nava, and Brian Lam.